TOWER HAMLETS PUBLIC LIBRARY

C001377732

A LUCKY LUKE ADVENTURE

APACHE CANYON

BY MORRIS & GOSCINNY

9th CINEBOOK
The 9th Art Publisher

D1421377

LONDON BOROUGH TOWER HAMLETS	
C00 137 7732	
HJ	31-Jul-2009
COMIC	£5.99
THCUB	

Original title: Lucky Luke – Canyon Apache

Original edition: © Dargaud Editeur Paris 1971 by Goscinny and Morris
© Lucky Comics
www.lucky-luke.com

Translator: Frederick W. Nolan
Lettering and text layout: Imadjinn sarl
Printed in Spain by Just Colour Graphic

This edition published in Great Britain in 2009 by
Cinebook Ltd
56 Beech Avenue
Canterbury, Kent
CT4 7TA
www.cinebook.com

A CIP catalogue record for this book
is available from the British Library

ISBN 978-1-905460-92-2

9th CINEBOOK
The 9th Art Publisher

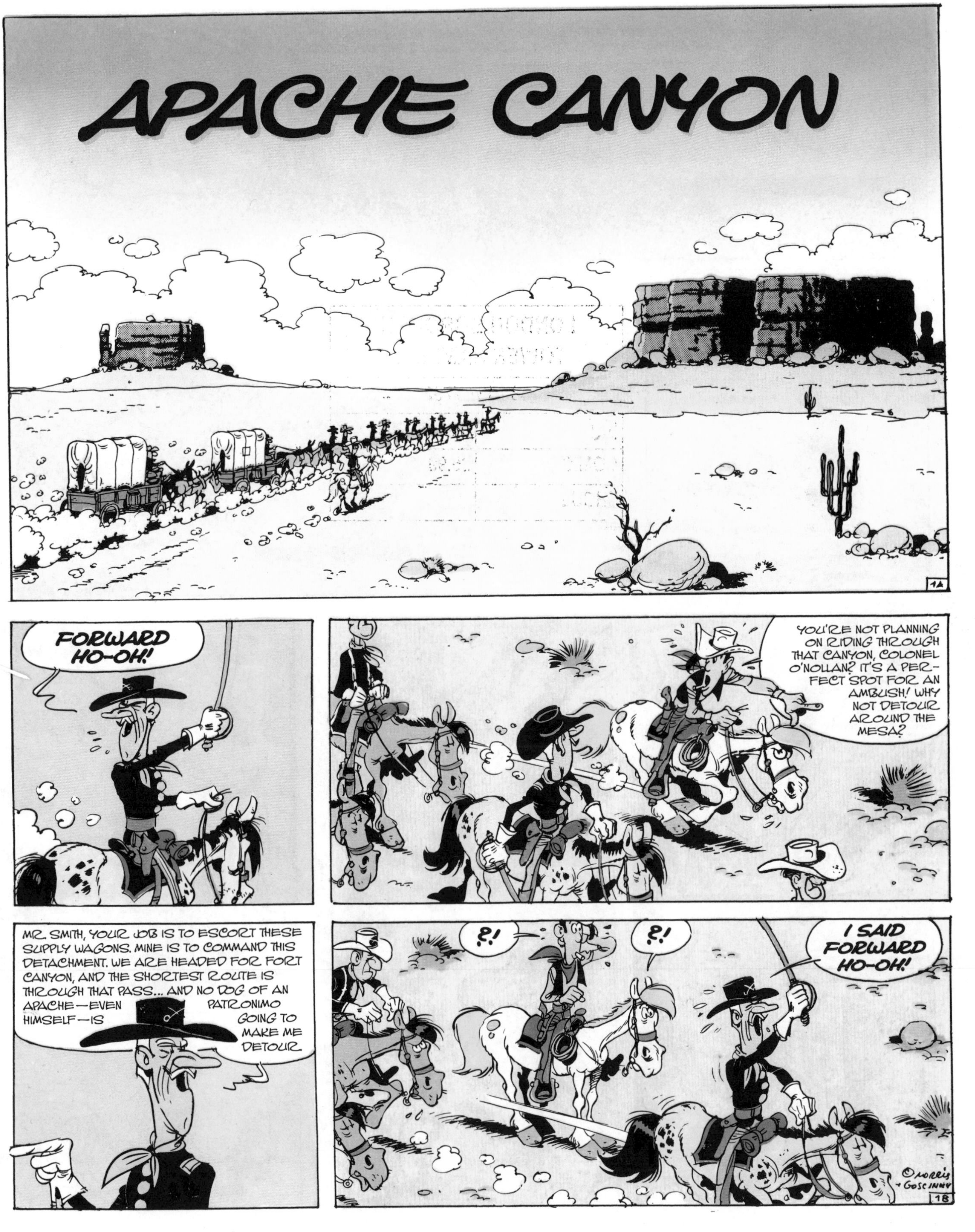
APACHE CANYON
FORWARD HO-OH!
YOU'RE NOT PLANNING ON RIDING THROUGH THAT CANYON, COLONEL O'NOLLAN? IT'S A PERFECT SPOT FOR AN AMBUSH! WHY NOT DETOUR AROUND THE MESA?
MR. SMITH, YOUR JOB IS TO ESCORT THESE SUPPLY WAGONS. MINE IS TO COMMAND THIS DETACHMENT. WE ARE HEADED FOR FORT CANYON, AND THE SHORTEST ROUTE IS THROUGH THAT PASS... AND NO DOG OF AN APACHE—EVEN PATRONIMO HIMSELF—IS GOING TO MAKE ME DETOUR.
?!
?!
I SAID FORWARD HO-OH!

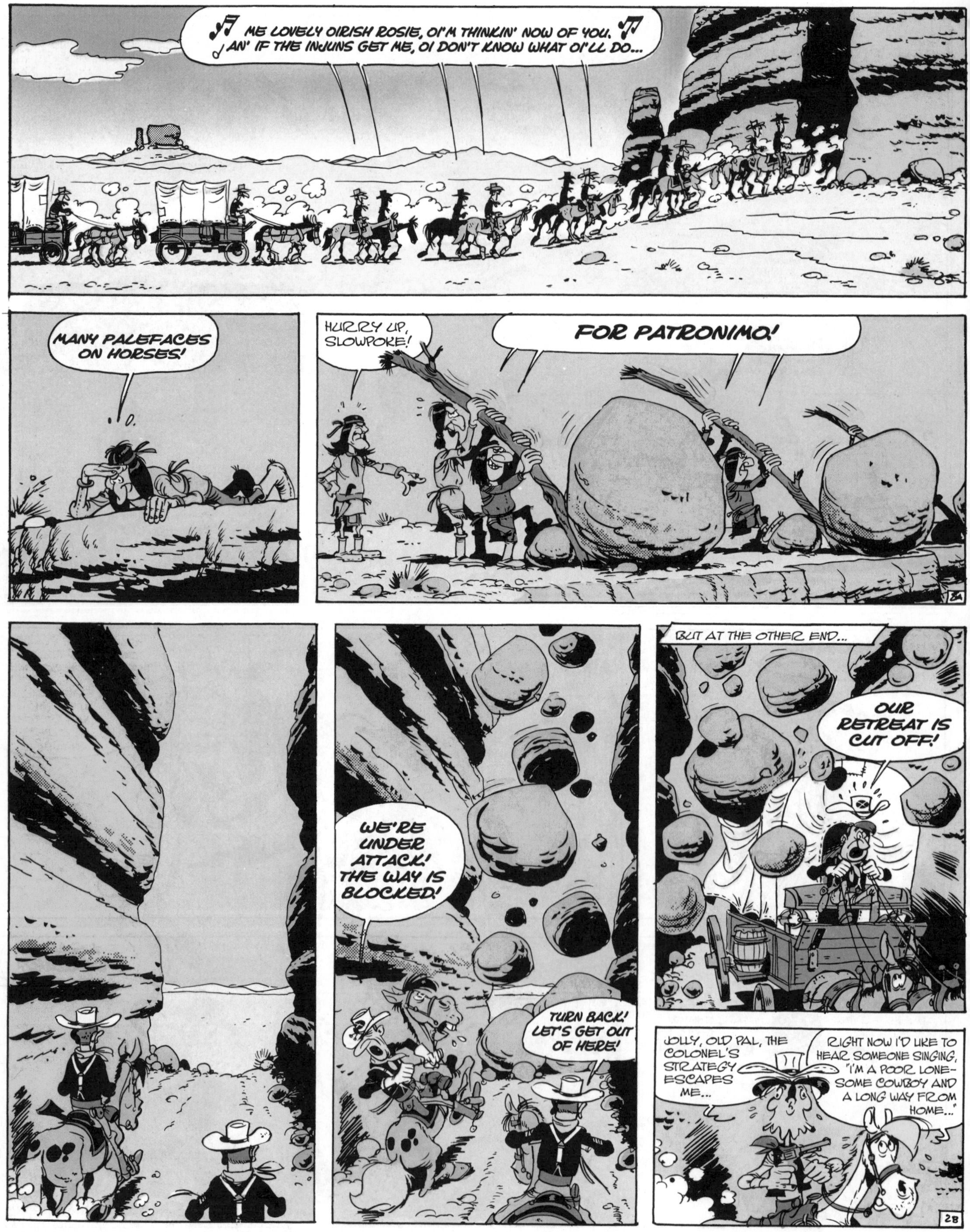
ME LOVELY OIRISH ROSIE, OI'M THINKIN' NOW OF YOU. AN' IF THE INJUNS GET ME, OI DON'T KNOW WHAT OI'LL DO...
MANY PALEFACES ON HORSES!
HURRY UP, SLOWPOKE!
FOR PATRONIMO!
WE'RE UNDER ATTACK! THE WAY IS BLOCKED!
TURN BACK! LET'S GET OUT OF HERE!
BUT AT THE OTHER END...
OUR RETREAT IS CUT OFF!
JOLLY, OLD PAL, THE COLONEL'S STRATEGY ESCAPES ME...
RIGHT NOW I'D LIKE TO HEAR SOMEONE SINGING, "I'M A POOR LONESOME COWBOY AND A LONG WAY FROM HOME..."

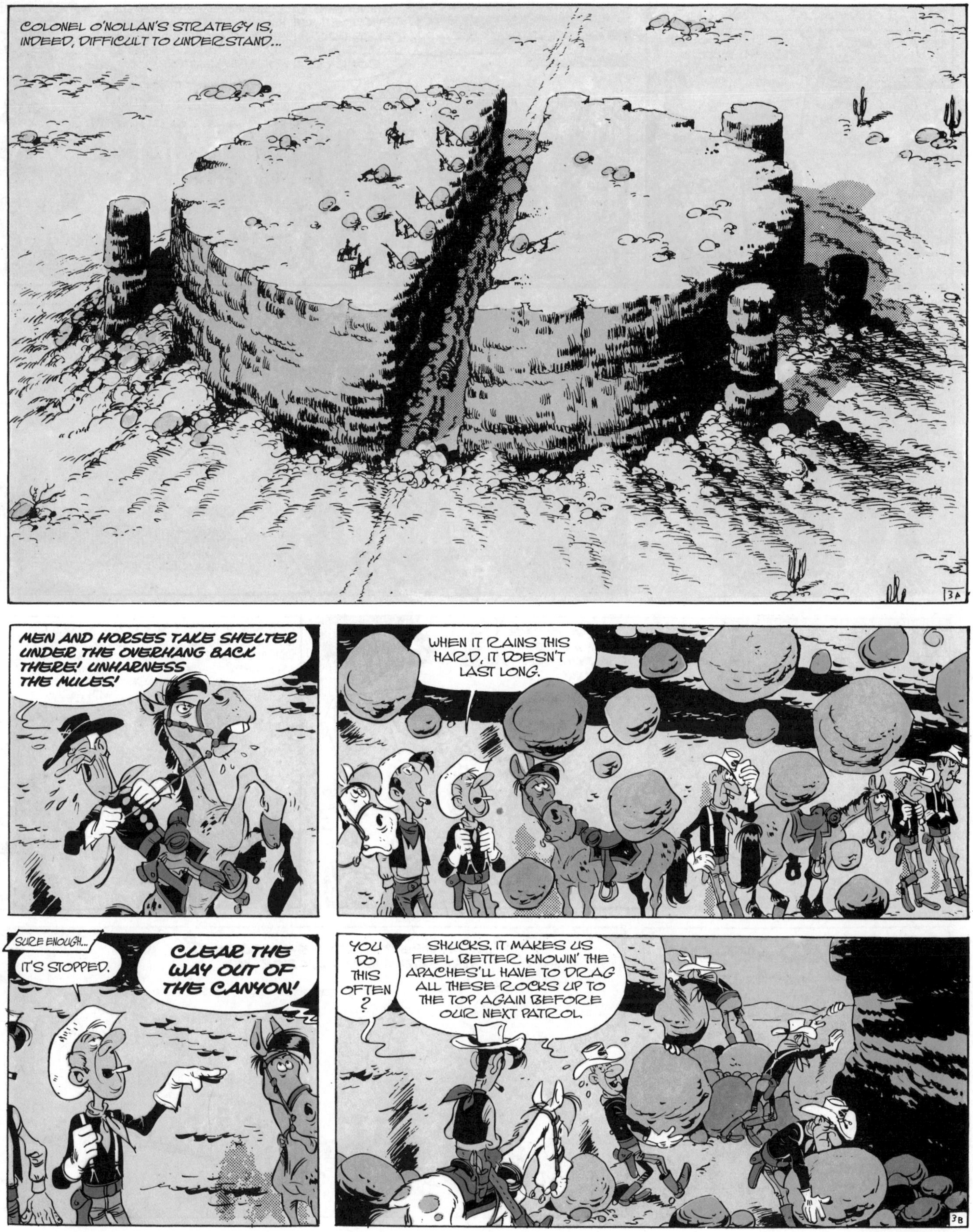
COLONEL O'NOLLAN'S STRATEGY IS, INDEED, DIFFICULT TO UNDERSTAND...
MEN AND HORSES TAKE SHELTER UNDER THE OVERHANG BACK THERE! UNHARNESS THE MULES!
WHEN IT RAINS THIS HARD, IT DOESN'T LAST LONG.
SURE ENOUGH...
IT'S STOPPED.
CLEAR THE WAY OUT OF THE CANYON!
YOU DO THIS OFTEN ?
SHUCKS. IT MAKES US FEEL BETTER KNOWIN' THE APACHES'LL HAVE TO DRAG ALL THESE ROCKS UP TO THE TOP AGAIN BEFORE OUR NEXT PATROL.

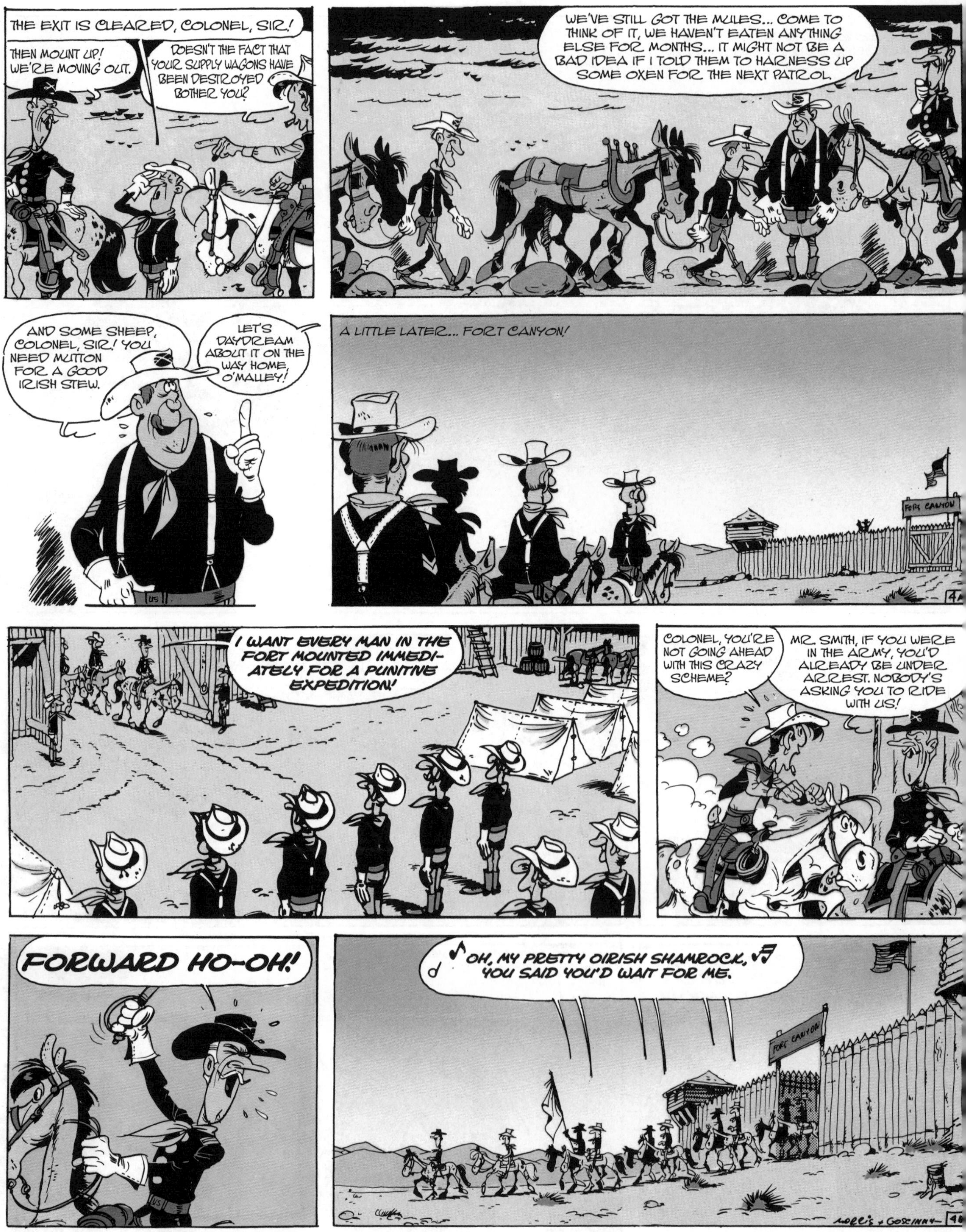
THE EXIT IS CLEARED, COLONEL, SIR!
THEN MOUNT UP! WE'RE MOVING OUT.
DOESN'T THE FACT THAT YOUR SUPPLY WAGONS HAVE BEEN DESTROYED BOTHER YOU?
WE'VE STILL GOT THE MULES... COME TO THINK OF IT, WE HAVEN'T EATEN ANYTHING ELSE FOR MONTHS... IT MIGHT NOT BE A BAD IDEA IF I TOLD THEM TO HARNESS UP SOME OXEN FOR THE NEXT PATROL.
AND SOME SHEEP, COLONEL, SIR! YOU NEED MUTTON FOR A GOOD IRISH STEW.
LET'S DAYDREAM ABOUT IT ON THE WAY HOME, O'MALLEY!
A LITTLE LATER... FORT CANYON!
FORT CANYON
I WANT EVERY MAN IN THE FORT MOUNTED IMMEDIATELY FOR A PUNITIVE EXPEDITION!
COLONEL, YOU'RE NOT GOING AHEAD WITH THIS CRAZY SCHEME?
MR. SMITH, IF YOU WERE IN THE ARMY, YOU'D ALREADY BE UNDER ARREST. NOBODY'S ASKING YOU TO RIDE WITH US!
FORWARD HO-OH!
OH, MY PRETTY OIRISH SHAMROCK, YOU SAID YOU'D WAIT FOR ME.
FORT CANYON
MORRIS + GOSCINNY

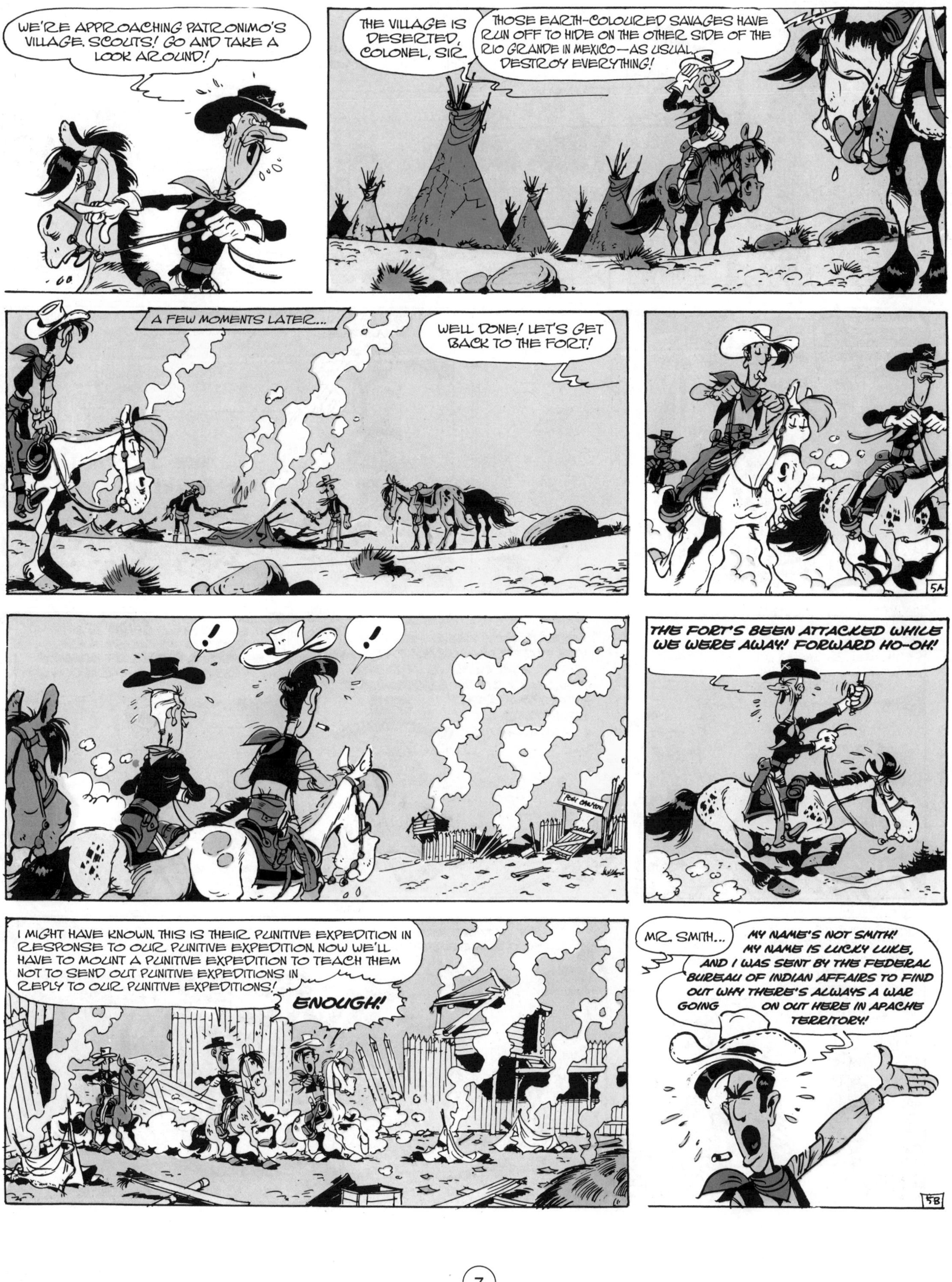
WE'RE APPROACHING PATRONIMO'S VILLAGE, SCOUTS! GO AND TAKE A LOOK AROUND!
THE VILLAGE IS DESERTED, COLONEL, SIR.
THOSE EARTH-COLOURED SAVAGES HAVE RUN OFF TO HIDE ON THE OTHER SIDE OF THE RIO GRANDE IN MEXICO—AS USUAL. DESTROY EVERYTHING!
A FEW MOMENTS LATER...
WELL DONE! LET'S GET BACK TO THE FORT!
!
!
THE FORT'S BEEN ATTACKED WHILE WE WERE AWAY! FORWARD HO-OH!
I MIGHT HAVE KNOWN. THIS IS THEIR PUNITIVE EXPEDITION IN RESPONSE TO OUR PUNITIVE EXPEDITION. NOW WE'LL HAVE TO MOUNT A PUNITIVE EXPEDITION TO TEACH THEM NOT TO SEND OUT PUNITIVE EXPEDITIONS IN REPLY TO OUR PUNITIVE EXPEDITIONS!
ENOUGH!
MR. SMITH...
MY NAME'S NOT SMITH! MY NAME IS LUCKY LUKE, AND I WAS SENT BY THE FEDERAL BUREAU OF INDIAN AFFAIRS TO FIND OUT WHY THERE'S ALWAYS A WAR GOING ON OUT HERE IN APACHE TERRITORY!

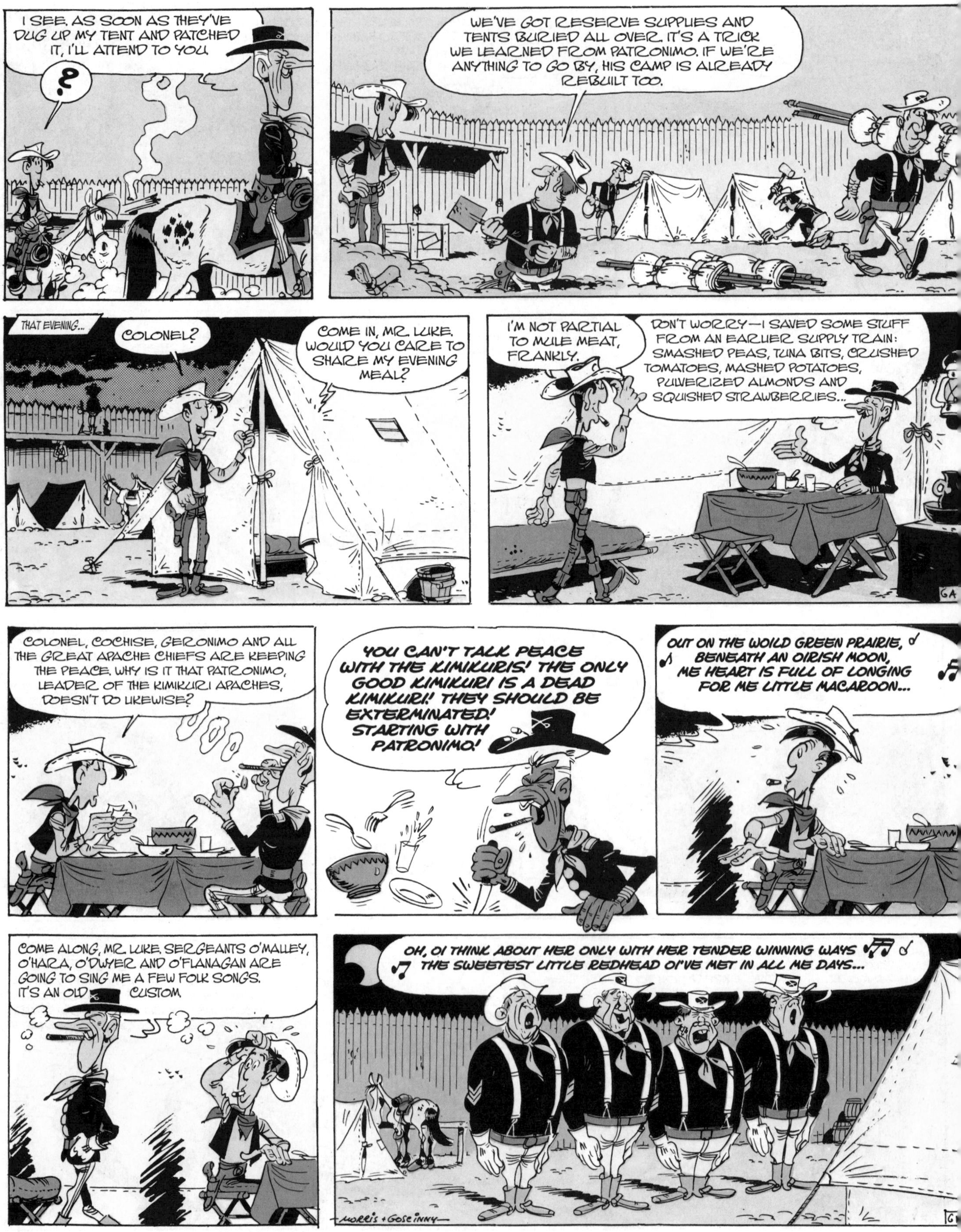
I SEE. AS SOON AS THEY'VE DUG UP MY TENT AND PATCHED IT, I'LL ATTEND TO YOU.
?
WE'VE GOT RESERVE SUPPLIES AND TENTS BURIED ALL OVER. IT'S A TRICK WE LEARNED FROM PATRONIMO. IF WE'RE ANYTHING TO GO BY, HIS CAMP IS ALREADY REBUILT TOO.
THAT EVENING...
COLONEL?
COME IN, MR. LUKE. WOULD YOU CARE TO SHARE MY EVENING MEAL?
I'M NOT PARTIAL TO MULE MEAT, FRANKLY.
DON'T WORRY—I SAVED SOME STUFF FROM AN EARLIER SUPPLY TRAIN: SMASHED PEAS, TUNA BITS, CRUSHED TOMATOES, MASHED POTATOES, PULVERIZED ALMONDS AND SQUISHED STRAWBERRIES...
COLONEL, COCHISE, GERONIMO AND ALL THE GREAT APACHE CHIEFS ARE KEEPING THE PEACE. WHY IS IT THAT PATRONIMO, LEADER OF THE KIMIKURI APACHES, DOESN'T DO LIKEWISE?
YOU CAN'T TALK PEACE WITH THE KIMIKURIS! THE ONLY GOOD KIMIKURI IS A DEAD KIMIKURI! THEY SHOULD BE EXTERMINATED! STARTING WITH PATRONIMO!
OUT ON THE WOILD GREEN PRAIRIE, BENEATH AN OIRISH MOON, ME HEART IS FULL OF LONGING FOR ME LITTLE MACAROON...
COME ALONG, MR. LUKE. SERGEANTS O'MALLEY, O'HARA, O'DWYER AND O'FLANAGAN ARE GOING TO SING ME A FEW FOLK SONGS. IT'S AN OLD CUSTOM.
OH, OI THINK ABOUT HER ONLY WITH HER TENDER WINNING WAYS THE SWEETEST LITTLE REDHEAD OI'VE MET IN ALL ME DAYS...
MORRIS + GOSCINNY

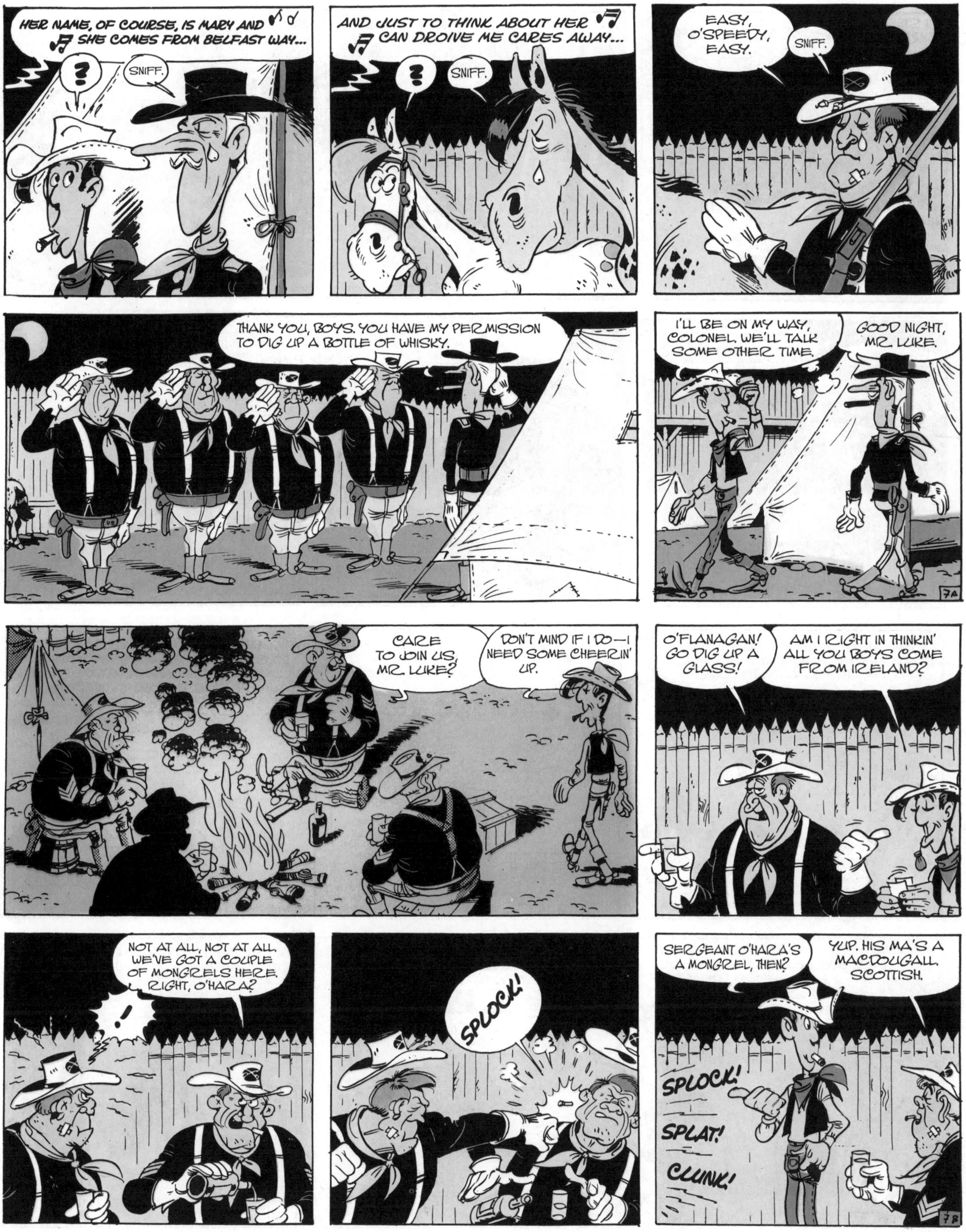
HER NAME, OF COURSE, IS MARY AND SHE COMES FROM BELFAST WAY...
?
SNIFF.
AND JUST TO THINK ABOUT HER CAN DROIVE ME CARES AWAY...
?
SNIFF.
EASY, O'SPEEDY, EASY.
SNIFF.
THANK YOU, BOYS. YOU HAVE MY PERMISSION TO DIG UP A BOTTLE OF WHISKY.
I'LL BE ON MY WAY, COLONEL. WE'LL TALK SOME OTHER TIME.
GOOD NIGHT, MR. LUKE.
CARE TO JOIN US, MR. LUKE?
DON'T MIND IF I DO—I NEED SOME CHEERIN' UP.
O'FLANAGAN! GO DIG UP A GLASS!
AM I RIGHT IN THINKIN' ALL YOU BOYS COME FROM IRELAND?
NOT AT ALL, NOT AT ALL. WE'VE GOT A COUPLE OF MONGRELS HERE. RIGHT, O'HARA?
!
SPLOCK!
SERGEANT O'HARA'S A MONGREL, THEN?
YUP. HIS MA'S A MACDOUGALL. SCOTTISH.
SPLOCK!
SPLAT!
CLUNK!

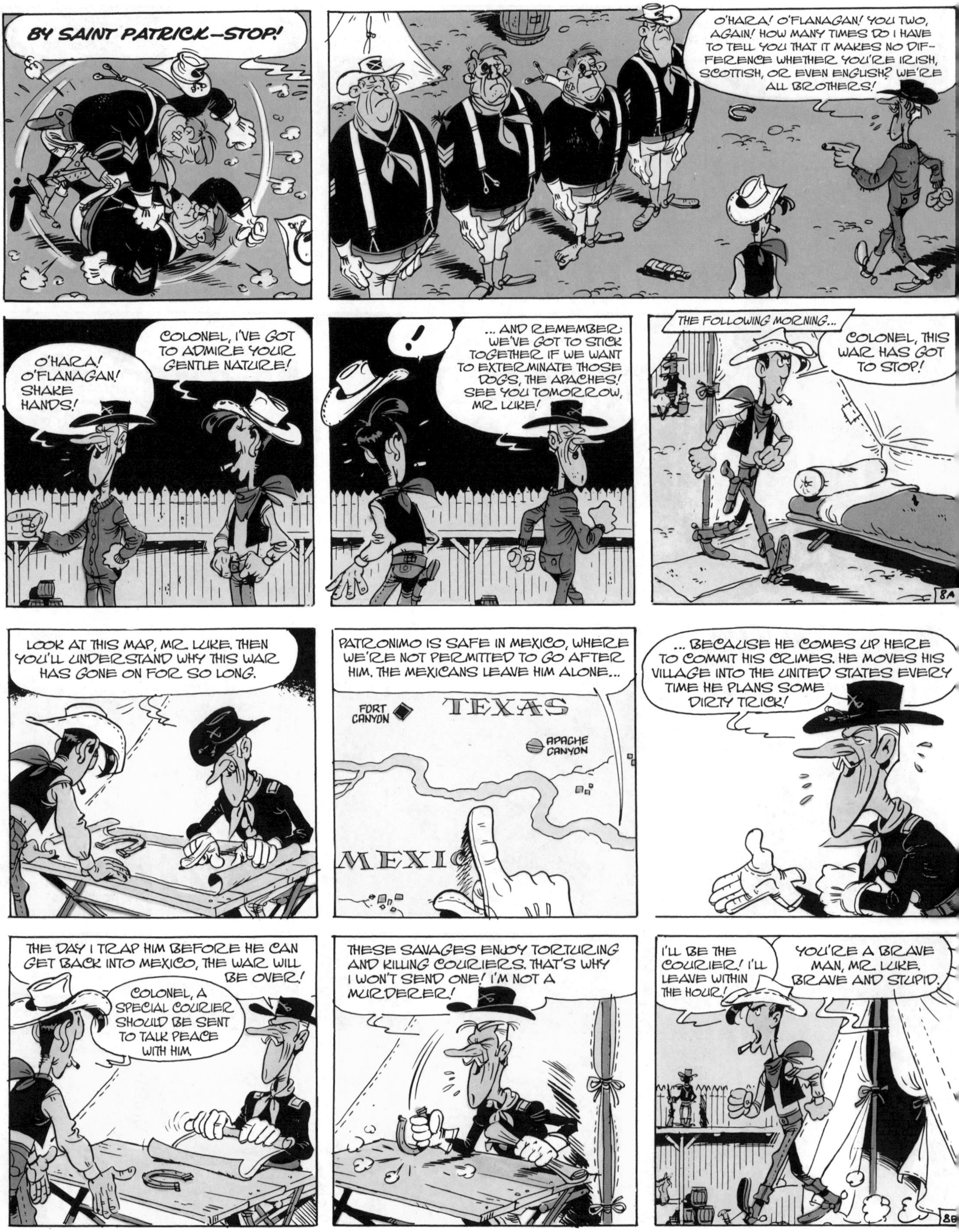
BY SAINT PATRICK—STOP!
O'HARA! O'FLANAGAN! YOU TWO, AGAIN! HOW MANY TIMES DO I HAVE TO TELL YOU THAT IT MAKES NO DIFFERENCE WHETHER YOU'RE IRISH, SCOTTISH, OR EVEN ENGLISH? WE'RE ALL BROTHERS!
O'HARA! O'FLANAGAN! SHAKE HANDS!
COLONEL, I'VE GOT TO ADMIRE YOUR GENTLE NATURE!
!
... AND REMEMBER: WE'VE GOT TO STICK TOGETHER IF WE WANT TO EXTERMINATE THOSE DOGS, THE APACHES! SEE YOU TOMORROW, MR. LUKE!
THE FOLLOWING MORNING...
COLONEL, THIS WAR HAS GOT TO STOP!
8A
LOOK AT THIS MAP, MR. LUKE. THEN YOU'LL UNDERSTAND WHY THIS WAR HAS GONE ON FOR SO LONG.
PATRONIMO IS SAFE IN MEXICO, WHERE WE'RE NOT PERMITTED TO GO AFTER HIM. THE MEXICANS LEAVE HIM ALONE...
FORT CANYON
TEXAS
APACHE CANYON
MEXI
... BECAUSE HE COMES UP HERE TO COMMIT HIS CRIMES. HE MOVES HIS VILLAGE INTO THE UNITED STATES EVERY TIME HE PLANS SOME DIRTY TRICK!
THE DAY I TRAP HIM BEFORE HE CAN GET BACK INTO MEXICO, THE WAR WILL BE OVER!
COLONEL, A SPECIAL COURIER SHOULD BE SENT TO TALK PEACE WITH HIM.
THESE SAVAGES ENJOY TORTURING AND KILLING COURIERS. THAT'S WHY I WON'T SEND ONE! I'M NOT A MURDERER!
I'LL BE THE COURIER! I'LL LEAVE WITHIN THE HOUR!
YOU'RE A BRAVE MAN, MR. LUKE. BRAVE AND STUPID.
8B

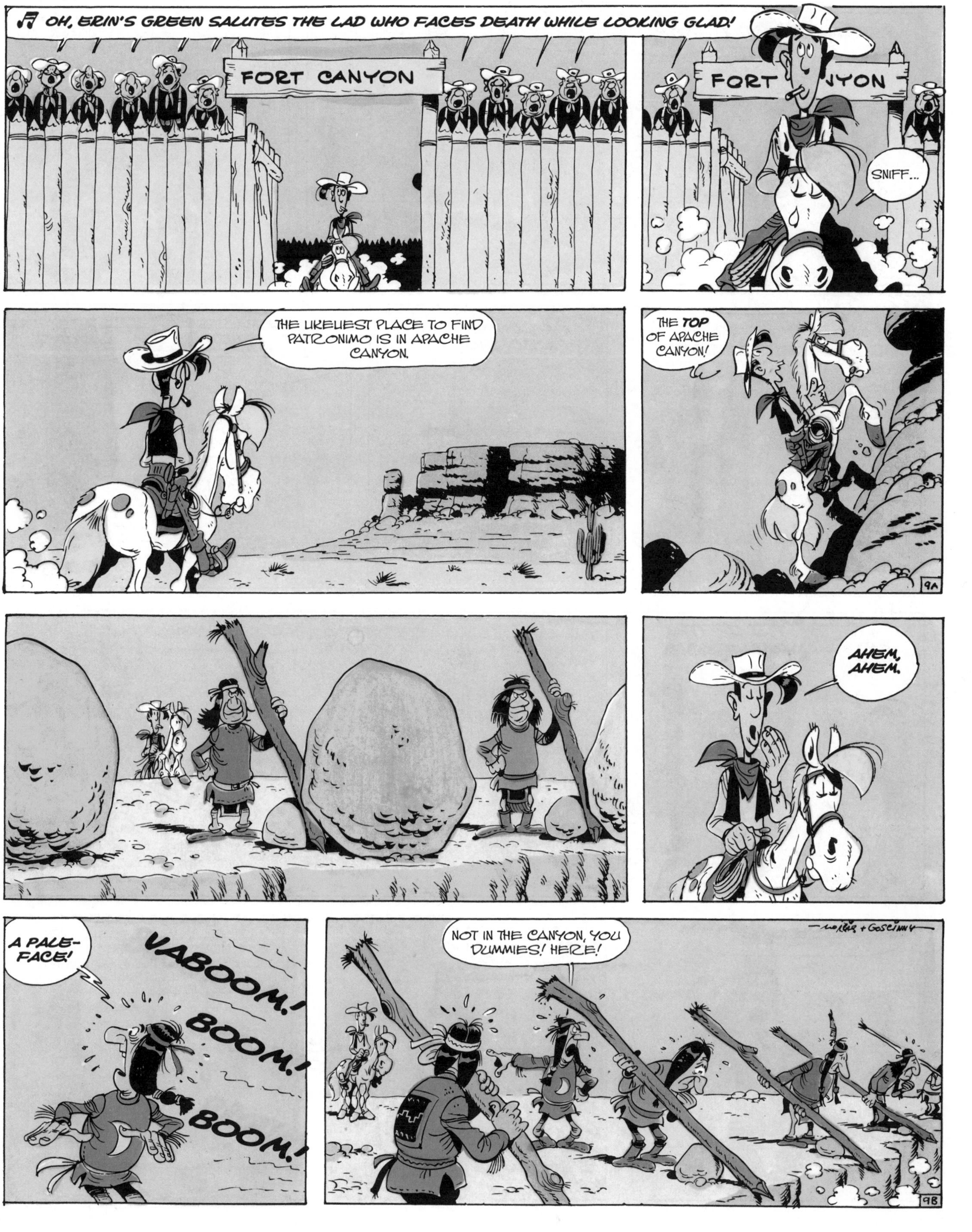
OH, ERIN'S GREEN SALUTES THE LAD WHO FACES DEATH WHILE LOOKING GLAD!
FORT CANYON
FORT ...NYON
SNIFF...
THE LIKELIEST PLACE TO FIND PATRONIMO IS IN APACHE CANYON.
THE TOP OF APACHE CANYON!
9A
AHEM, AHEM.
A PALE-FACE!
VABOOM!
BOOM!
BOOM!
MORRIS + GOSCINNY
NOT IN THE CANYON, YOU DUMMIES! HERE!
9B

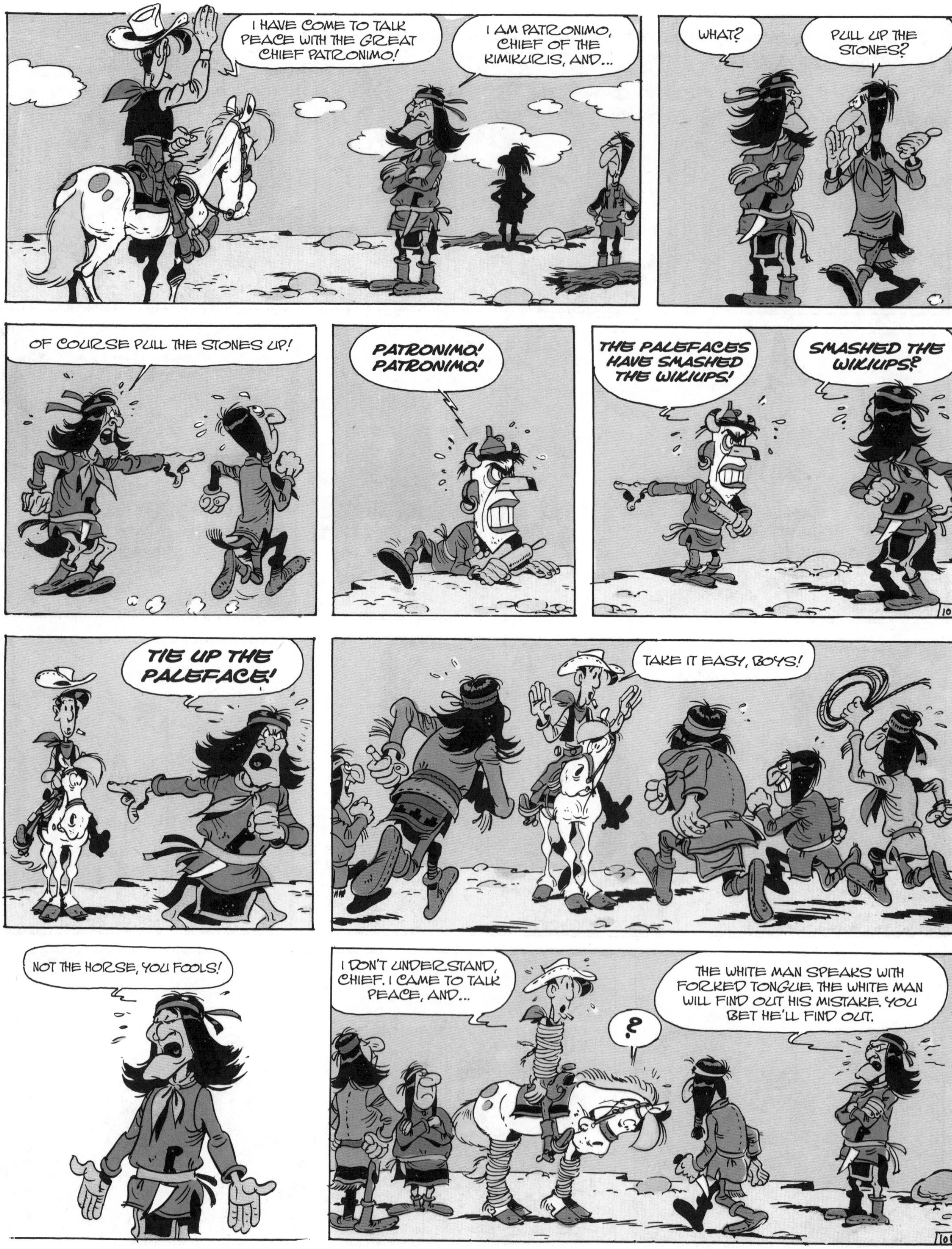
I HAVE COME TO TALK PEACE WITH THE GREAT CHIEF PATRONIMO!
I AM PATRONIMO, CHIEF OF THE KIMIKURIS, AND...
WHAT?
PULL UP THE STONES?
OF COURSE PULL THE STONES UP!
PATRONIMO! PATRONIMO!
THE PALEFACES HAVE SMASHED THE WIKIUPS!
SMASHED THE WIKIUPS?
10A
TIE UP THE PALEFACE!
TAKE IT EASY, BOYS!
NOT THE HORSE, YOU FOOLS!
I DON'T UNDERSTAND, CHIEF. I CAME TO TALK PEACE, AND...
?
THE WHITE MAN SPEAKS WITH FORKED TONGUE. THE WHITE MAN WILL FIND OUT HIS MISTAKE. YOU BET HE'LL FIND OUT.
10B

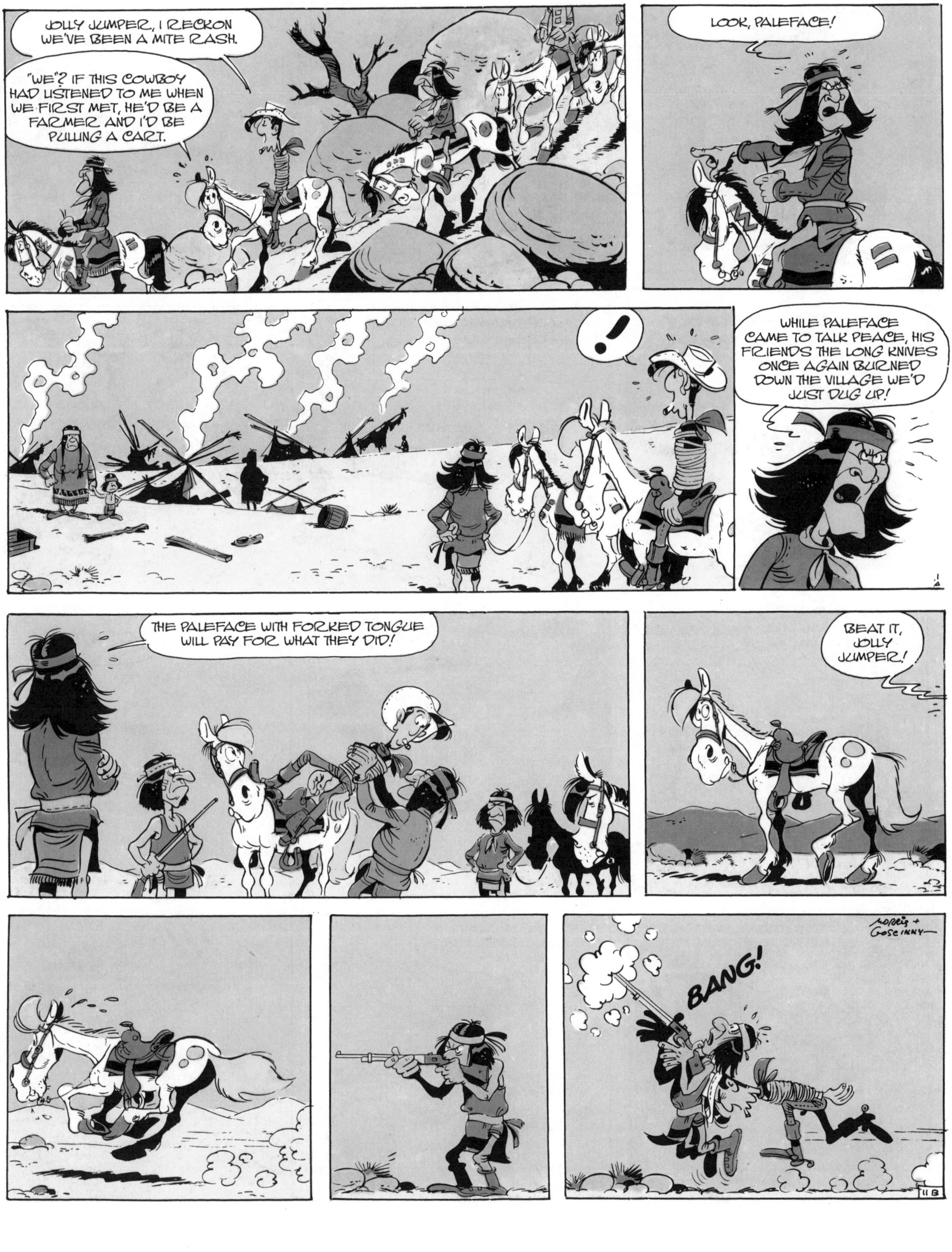
JOLLY JUMPER, I RECKON WE'VE BEEN A MITE RASH.
"WE"? IF THIS COWBOY HAD LISTENED TO ME WHEN WE FIRST MET, HE'D BE A FARMER AND I'D BE PULLING A CART.
LOOK, PALEFACE!
!
WHILE PALEFACE CAME TO TALK PEACE, HIS FRIENDS THE LONG KNIVES ONCE AGAIN BURNED DOWN THE VILLAGE WE'D JUST DUG UP!
THE PALEFACE WITH FORKED TONGUE WILL PAY FOR WHAT THEY DID!
BEAT IT, JOLLY JUMPER!
MORRIS + GOSCINNY
BANG!

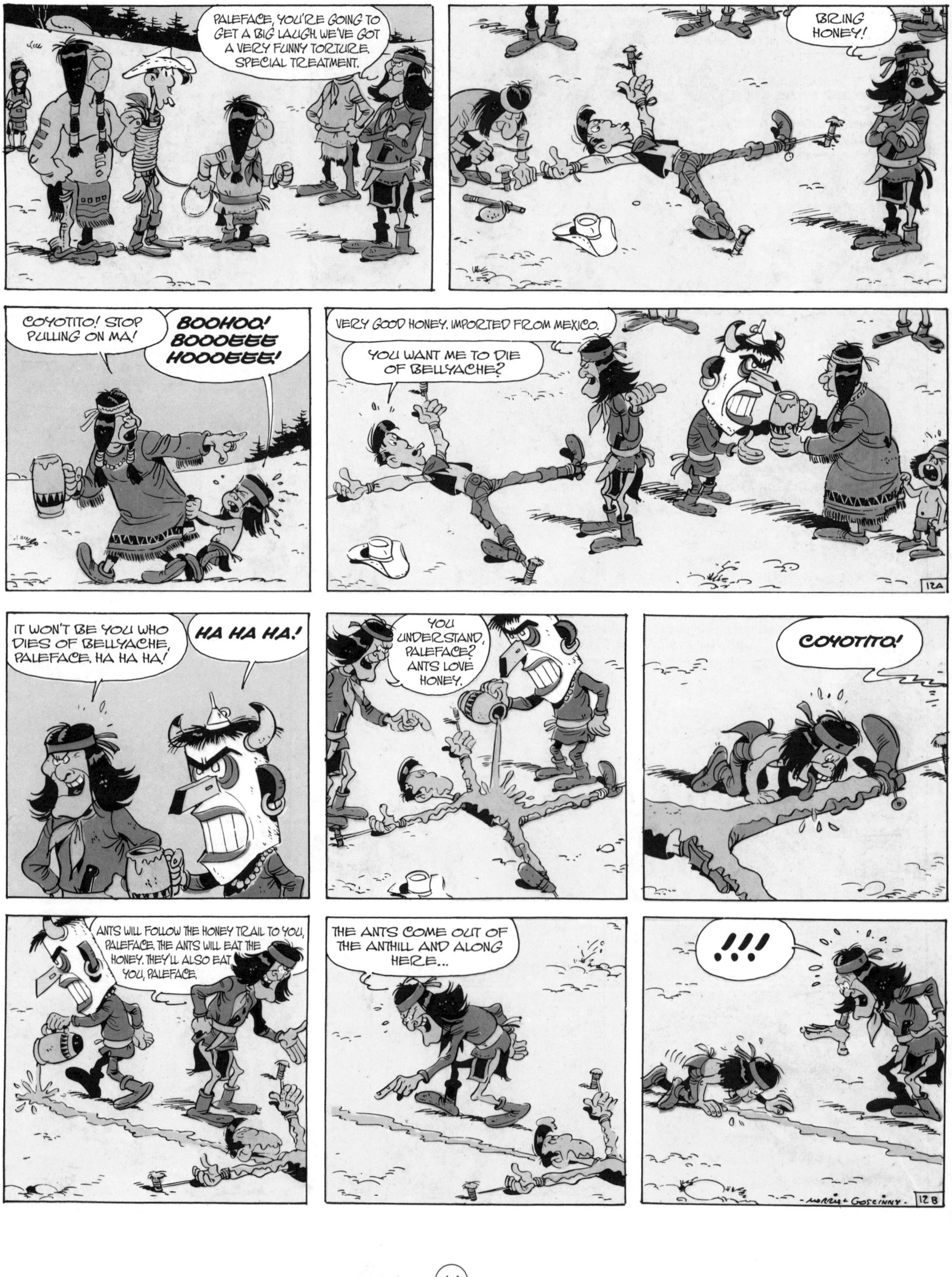

PALEFACE, YOU'RE GOING TO GET A BIG LAUGH. WE'VE GOT A VERY FUNNY TORTURE. SPECIAL TREATMENT.
BRING HONEY!
COYOTITO! STOP PULLING ON MA!
BOOHOO! BOOOEEE HOOOEEE!
VERY GOOD HONEY. IMPORTED FROM MEXICO.
YOU WANT ME TO DIE OF BELLYACHE?
12A
IT WON'T BE YOU WHO DIES OF BELLYACHE, PALEFACE. HA HA HA!
HA HA HA!
YOU UNDERSTAND, PALEFACE? ANTS LOVE HONEY.
COYOTITO!
ANTS WILL FOLLOW THE HONEY TRAIL TO YOU, PALEFACE. THE ANTS WILL EAT THE HONEY. THEY'LL ALSO EAT YOU, PALEFACE.
THE ANTS COME OUT OF THE ANTHILL AND ALONG HERE...
!!!
MORRIS + GOSCINNY
12B

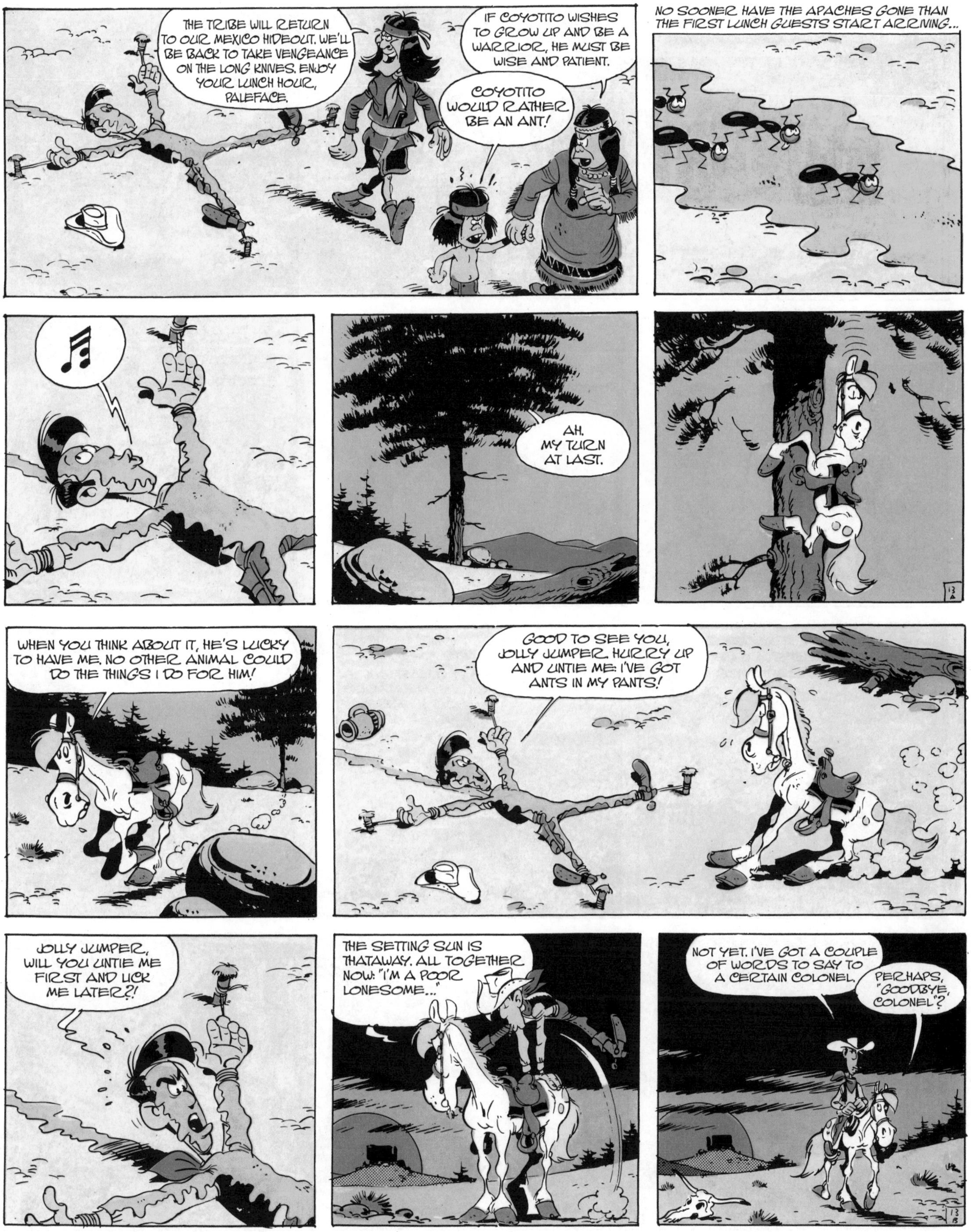
THE TRIBE WILL RETURN TO OUR MEXICO HIDEOUT. WE'LL BE BACK TO TAKE VENGEANCE ON THE LONG KNIVES. ENJOY YOUR LUNCH HOUR, PALEFACE.
IF COYOTITO WISHES TO GROW UP AND BE A WARRIOR, HE MUST BE WISE AND PATIENT.
COYOTITO WOULD RATHER BE AN ANT!
NO SOONER HAVE THE APACHES GONE THAN THE FIRST LUNCH GUESTS START ARRIVING...
AH. MY TURN AT LAST.
WHEN YOU THINK ABOUT IT, HE'S LUCKY TO HAVE ME. NO OTHER ANIMAL COULD DO THE THINGS I DO FOR HIM!
GOOD TO SEE YOU, JOLLY JUMPER. HURRY UP AND UNTIE ME: I'VE GOT ANTS IN MY PANTS!
JOLLY JUMPER, WILL YOU UNTIE ME FIRST AND LICK ME LATER?!
THE SETTING SUN IS THATAWAY. ALL TOGETHER NOW: "I'M A POOR LONESOME..."
NOT YET. I'VE GOT A COUPLE OF WORDS TO SAY TO A CERTAIN COLONEL.
PERHAPS, "GOODBYE, COLONEL"?

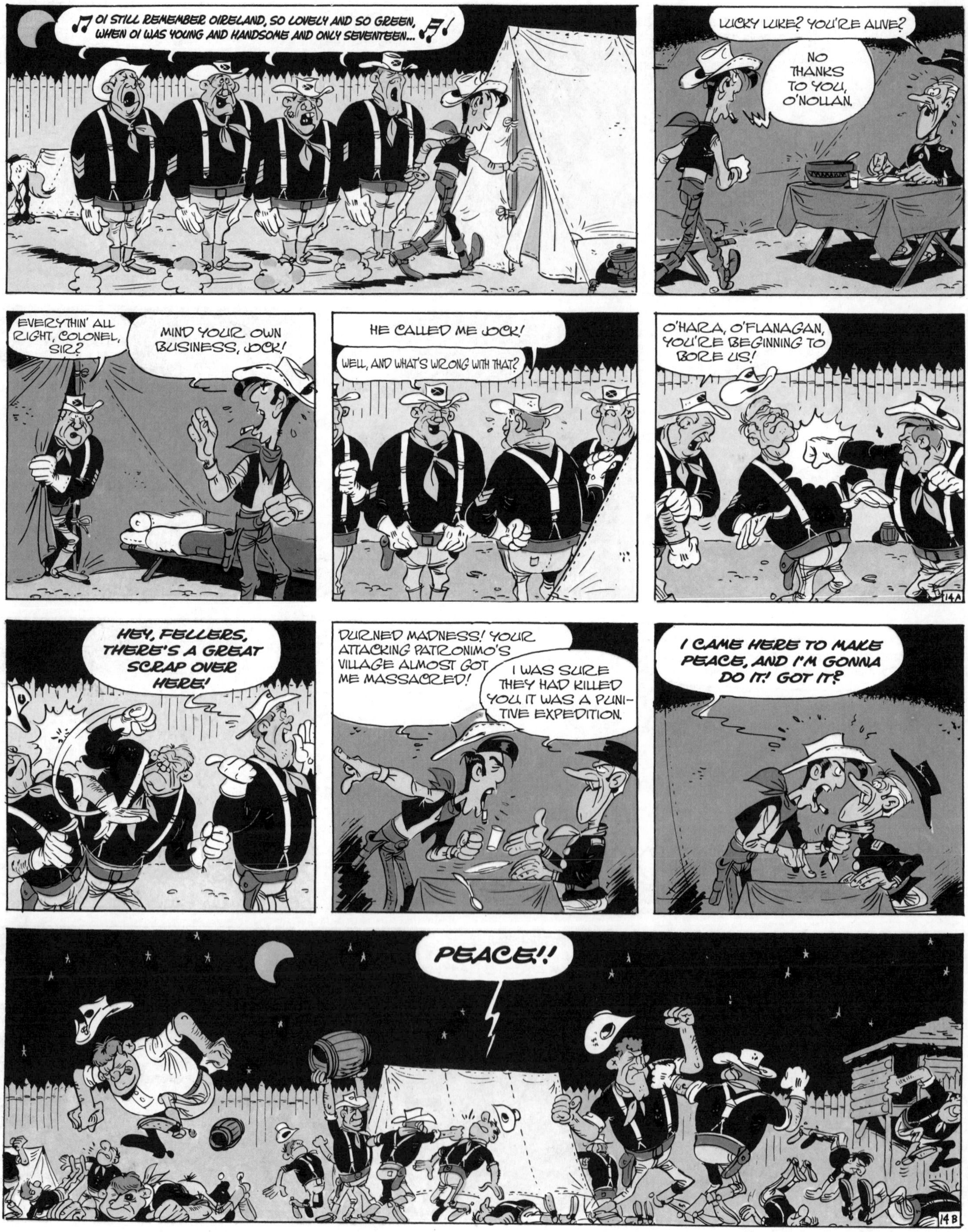
♫ OI STILL REMEMBER OIRELAND, SO LOVELY AND SO GREEN, WHEN OI WAS YOUNG AND HANDSOME AND ONLY SEVENTEEN... ♫!
LUCKY LUKE? YOU'RE ALIVE?
NO THANKS TO YOU, O'NOLLAN.
EVERYTHIN' ALL RIGHT, COLONEL, SIR?
MIND YOUR OWN BUSINESS, JOCK!
HE CALLED ME JOCK!
WELL, AND WHAT'S WRONG WITH THAT?
O'HARA, O'FLANAGAN, YOU'RE BEGINNING TO BORE US!
14A
HEY, FELLERS, THERE'S A GREAT SCRAP OVER HERE!
DURNED MADNESS! YOUR ATTACKING PATRONIMO'S VILLAGE ALMOST GOT ME MASSACRED!
I WAS SURE THEY HAD KILLED YOU. IT WAS A PUNITIVE EXPEDITION.
I CAME HERE TO MAKE PEACE, AND I'M GONNA DO IT! GOT IT?
PEACE!!
14B

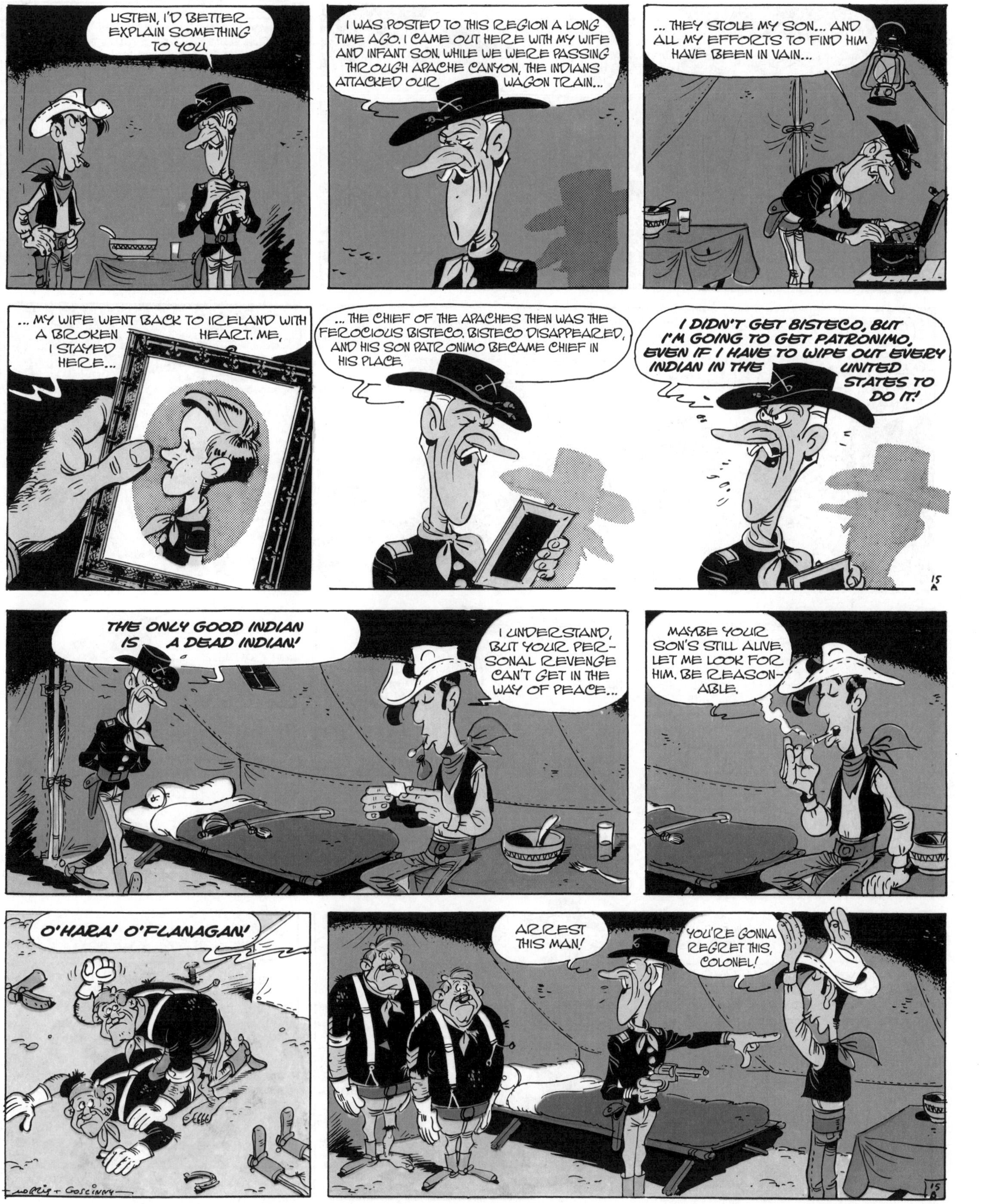

LISTEN, I'D BETTER EXPLAIN SOMETHING TO YOU.
I WAS POSTED TO THIS REGION A LONG TIME AGO. I CAME OUT HERE WITH MY WIFE AND INFANT SON. WHILE WE WERE PASSING THROUGH APACHE CANYON, THE INDIANS ATTACKED OUR WAGON TRAIN...
... THEY STOLE MY SON... AND ALL MY EFFORTS TO FIND HIM HAVE BEEN IN VAIN...
... MY WIFE WENT BACK TO IRELAND WITH A BROKEN HEART. ME, I STAYED HERE...
... THE CHIEF OF THE APACHES THEN WAS THE FEROCIOUS BISTECO. BISTECO DISAPPEARED, AND HIS SON PATRONIMO BECAME CHIEF IN HIS PLACE.
I DIDN'T GET BISTECO, BUT I'M GOING TO GET PATRONIMO, EVEN IF I HAVE TO WIPE OUT EVERY INDIAN IN THE UNITED STATES TO DO IT!
THE ONLY GOOD INDIAN IS A DEAD INDIAN!
I UNDERSTAND, BUT YOUR PERSONAL REVENGE CAN'T GET IN THE WAY OF PEACE...
MAYBE YOUR SON'S STILL ALIVE. LET ME LOOK FOR HIM. BE REASONABLE.
O'HARA! O'FLANAGAN!
ARREST THIS MAN!
YOU'RE GONNA REGRET THIS, COLONEL!
MORRIS + GOSCINNY

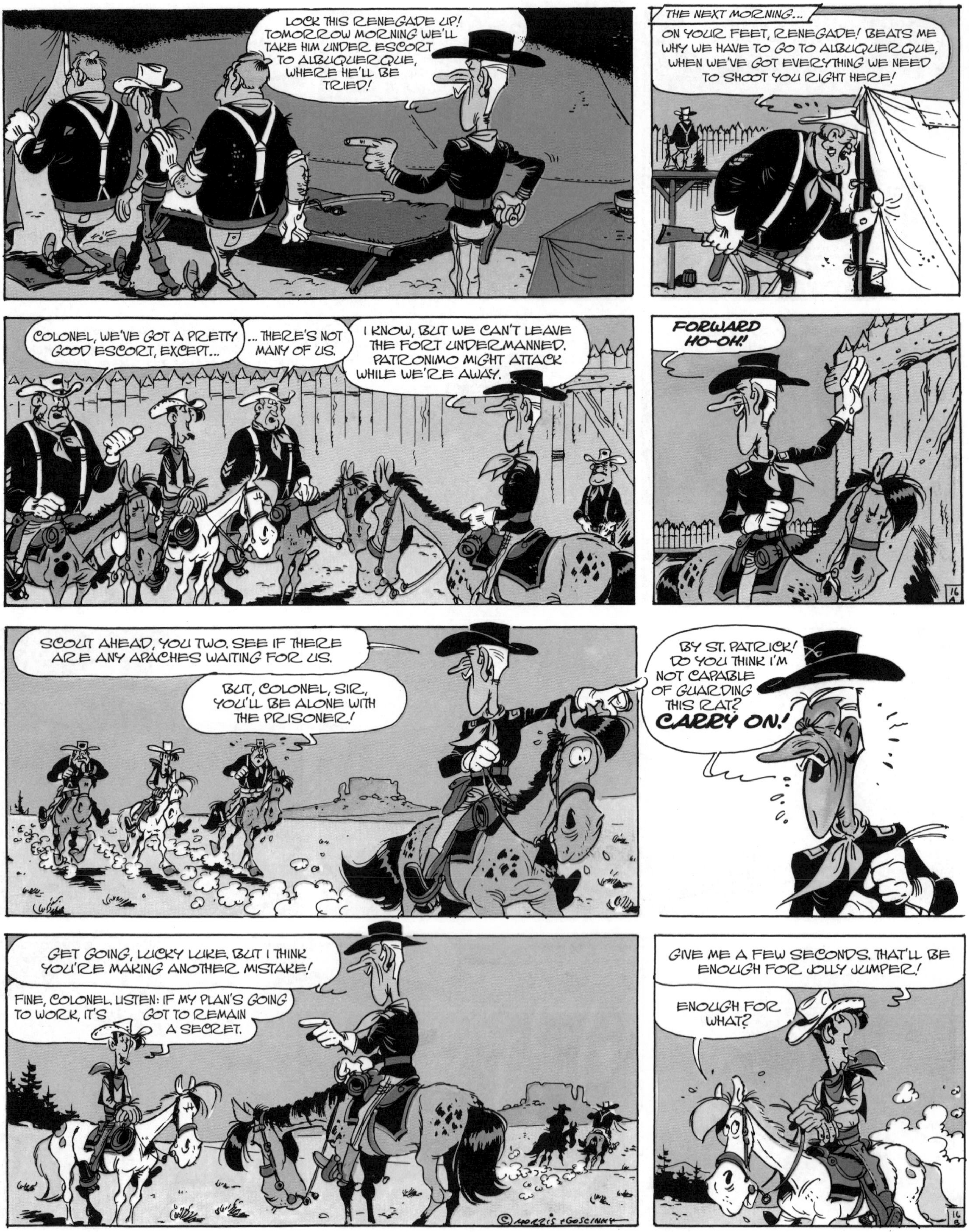
LOCK THIS RENEGADE UP! TOMORROW MORNING WE'LL TAKE HIM UNDER ESCORT TO ALBUQUERQUE, WHERE HE'LL BE TRIED!
THE NEXT MORNING...
ON YOUR FEET, RENEGADE! BEATS ME WHY WE HAVE TO GO TO ALBUQUERQUE, WHEN WE'VE GOT EVERYTHING WE NEED TO SHOOT YOU RIGHT HERE!
COLONEL, WE'VE GOT A PRETTY GOOD ESCORT, EXCEPT...
... THERE'S NOT MANY OF US.
I KNOW, BUT WE CAN'T LEAVE THE FORT UNDERMANNED. PATRONIMO MIGHT ATTACK WHILE WE'RE AWAY.
FORWARD HO-OH!
SCOUT AHEAD, YOU TWO. SEE IF THERE ARE ANY APACHES WAITING FOR US.
BUT, COLONEL, SIR, YOU'LL BE ALONE WITH THE PRISONER!
BY ST. PATRICK! DO YOU THINK I'M NOT CAPABLE OF GUARDING THIS RAT? CARRY ON!
GET GOING, LUCKY LUKE. BUT I THINK YOU'RE MAKING ANOTHER MISTAKE!
FINE, COLONEL. LISTEN: IF MY PLAN'S GOING TO WORK, IT'S GOT TO REMAIN A SECRET.
GIVE ME A FEW SECONDS. THAT'LL BE ENOUGH FOR JOLLY JUMPER!
ENOUGH FOR WHAT?
© MORRIS + GOSCINNY

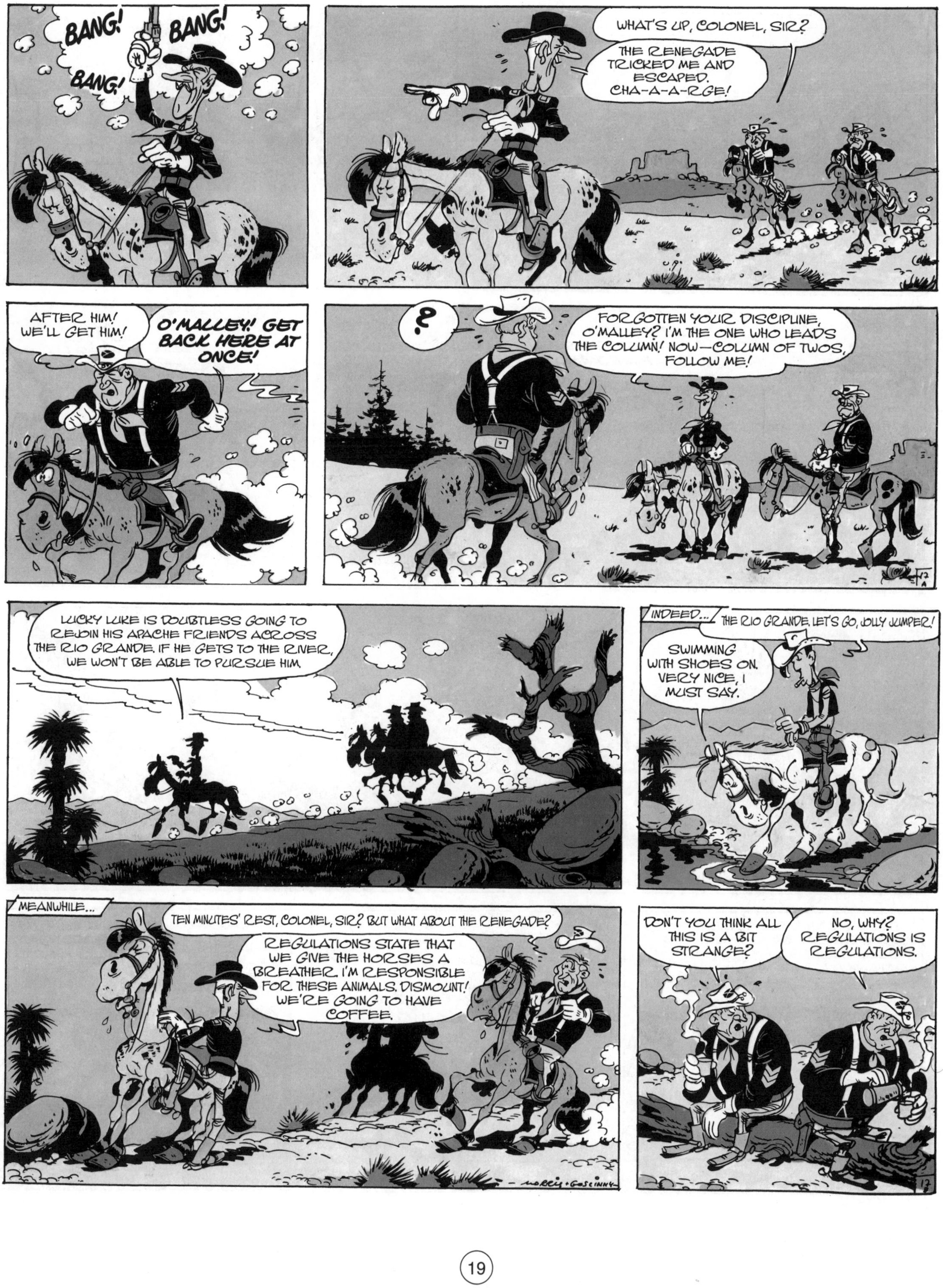

BANG! BANG! BANG!
WHAT'S UP, COLONEL, SIR?
THE RENEGADE TRICKED ME AND ESCAPED. CHA-A-A-RGE!
AFTER HIM! WE'LL GET HIM!
O'MALLEY! GET BACK HERE AT ONCE!
?
FORGOTTEN YOUR DISCIPLINE, O'MALLEY? I'M THE ONE WHO LEADS THE COLUMN! NOW—COLUMN OF TWOS, FOLLOW ME!
LUCKY LUKE IS DOUBTLESS GOING TO REJOIN HIS APACHE FRIENDS ACROSS THE RIO GRANDE. IF HE GETS TO THE RIVER, WE WON'T BE ABLE TO PURSUE HIM.
INDEED...
THE RIO GRANDE. LET'S GO, JOLLY JUMPER!
SWIMMING WITH SHOES ON. VERY NICE, I MUST SAY.
MEANWHILE...
TEN MINUTES' REST, COLONEL, SIR? BUT WHAT ABOUT THE RENEGADE?
REGULATIONS STATE THAT WE GIVE THE HORSES A BREATHER. I'M RESPONSIBLE FOR THESE ANIMALS. DISMOUNT! WE'RE GOING TO HAVE COFFEE.
DON'T YOU THINK ALL THIS IS A BIT STRANGE?
NO, WHY? REGULATIONS IS REGULATIONS.

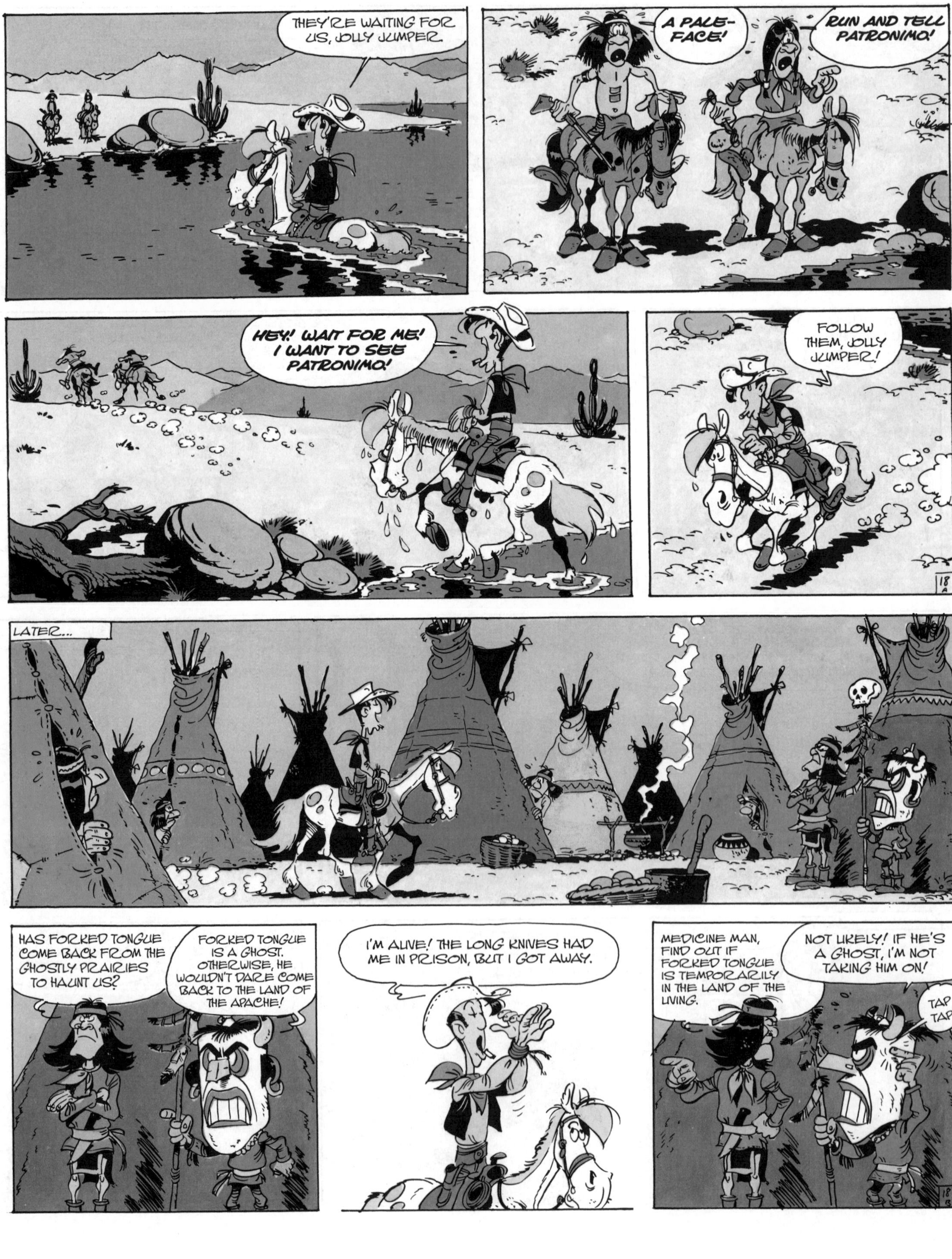
THEY'RE WAITING FOR US, JOLLY JUMPER.
A PALE-FACE!
RUN AND TELL PATRONIMO!
HEY! WAIT FOR ME! I WANT TO SEE PATRONIMO!
FOLLOW THEM, JOLLY JUMPER!
LATER...
HAS FORKED TONGUE COME BACK FROM THE GHOSTLY PRAIRIES TO HAUNT US?
FORKED TONGUE IS A GHOST. OTHERWISE, HE WOULDN'T DARE COME BACK TO THE LAND OF THE APACHE!
I'M ALIVE! THE LONG KNIVES HAD ME IN PRISON, BUT I GOT AWAY.
MEDICINE MAN, FIND OUT IF FORKED TONGUE IS TEMPORARILY IN THE LAND OF THE LIVING.
NOT LIKELY! IF HE'S A GHOST, I'M NOT TAKING HIM ON!
TAP TAP

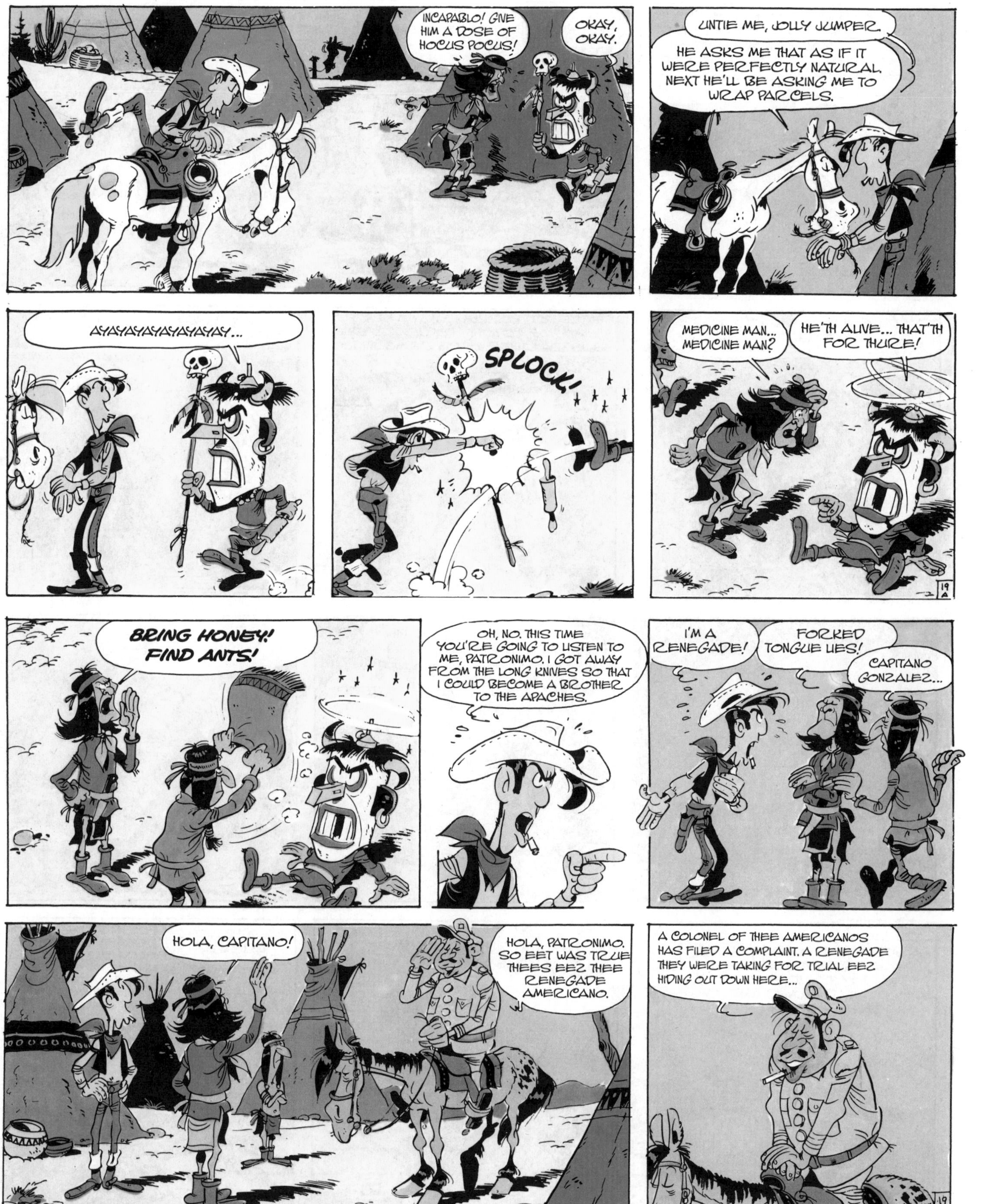
INCAPABLO! GIVE HIM A DOSE OF HOCUS POCUS!
OKAY, OKAY.
UNTIE ME, JOLLY JUMPER.
HE ASKS ME THAT AS IF IT WERE PERFECTLY NATURAL. NEXT HE'LL BE ASKING ME TO WRAP PARCELS.
AYAYAYAYAYAYAYAYAY...
SPLOCK!
MEDICINE MAN... MEDICINE MAN?
HE'TH ALIVE... THAT'TH FOR THURE!
BRING HONEY! FIND ANTS!
OH, NO. THIS TIME YOU'RE GOING TO LISTEN TO ME, PATRONIMO. I GOT AWAY FROM THE LONG KNIVES SO THAT I COULD BECOME A BROTHER TO THE APACHES.
I'M A RENEGADE!
FORKED TONGUE LIES!
CAPITANO GONZALEZ...
HOLA, CAPITANO!
HOLA, PATRONIMO. SO EET WAS TRUE THEES EEZ THEE RENEGADE AMERICANO.
A COLONEL OF THEE AMERICANOS HAS FILED A COMPLAINT. A RENEGADE THEY WERE TAKING FOR TRIAL EEZ HIDING OUT DOWN HERE...

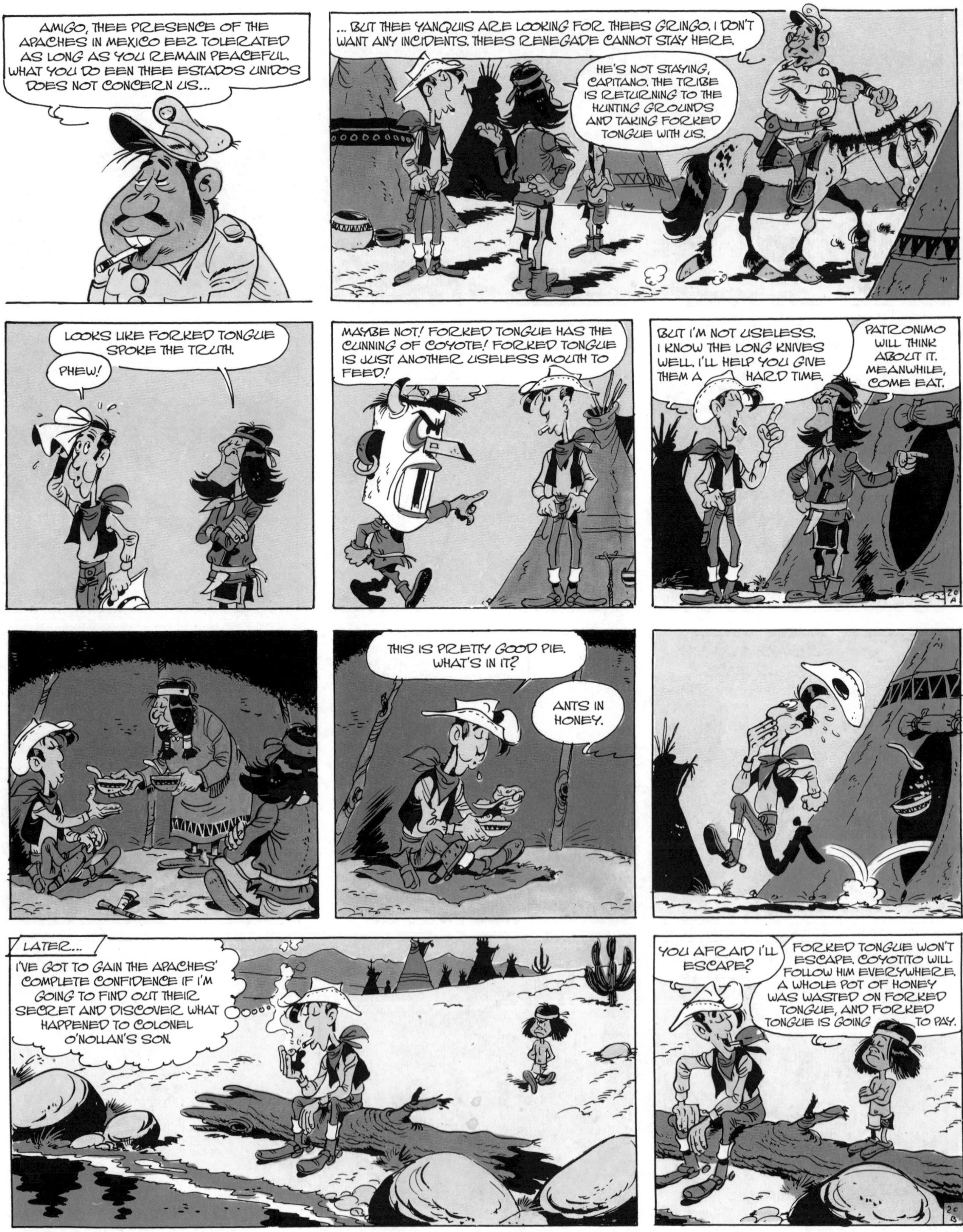
AMIGO, THEE PRESENCE OF THE APACHES IN MEXICO EEZ TOLERATED AS LONG AS YOU REMAIN PEACEFUL. WHAT YOU DO EEN THEE ESTADOS UNIDOS DOES NOT CONCERN US...
... BUT THEE YANQUIS ARE LOOKING FOR THEES GRINGO. I DON'T WANT ANY INCIDENTS. THEES RENEGADE CANNOT STAY HERE.
HE'S NOT STAYING, CAPITANO. THE TRIBE IS RETURNING TO THE HUNTING GROUNDS AND TAKING FORKED TONGUE WITH US.
LOOKS LIKE FORKED TONGUE SPOKE THE TRUTH.
PHEW!
MAYBE NOT! FORKED TONGUE HAS THE CUNNING OF COYOTE! FORKED TONGUE IS JUST ANOTHER USELESS MOUTH TO FEED!
BUT I'M NOT USELESS. I KNOW THE LONG KNIVES WELL. I'LL HELP YOU GIVE THEM A HARD TIME.
PATRONIMO WILL THINK ABOUT IT. MEANWHILE, COME EAT.
THIS IS PRETTY GOOD PIE. WHAT'S IN IT?
ANTS IN HONEY.
LATER...
I'VE GOT TO GAIN THE APACHES' COMPLETE CONFIDENCE IF I'M GOING TO FIND OUT THEIR SECRET AND DISCOVER WHAT HAPPENED TO COLONEL O'NOLLAN'S SON.
YOU AFRAID I'LL ESCAPE?
FORKED TONGUE WON'T ESCAPE. COYOTITO WILL FOLLOW HIM EVERYWHERE. A WHOLE POT OF HONEY WAS WASTED ON FORKED TONGUE, AND FORKED TONGUE IS GOING TO PAY.

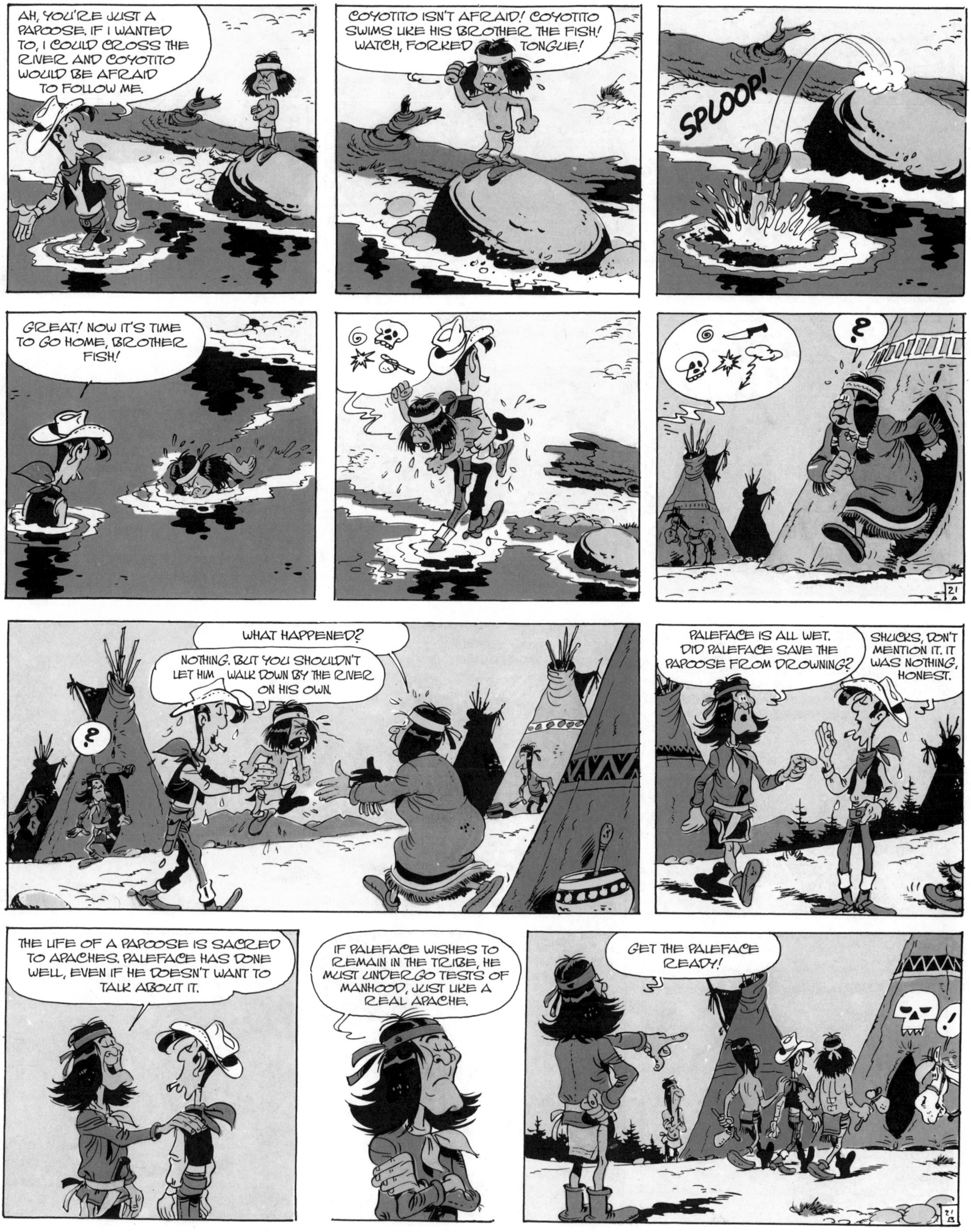
AH, YOU'RE JUST A PAPOOSE. IF I WANTED TO, I COULD CROSS THE RIVER AND COYOTITO WOULD BE AFRAID TO FOLLOW ME.
COYOTITO ISN'T AFRAID! COYOTITO SWIMS LIKE HIS BROTHER THE FISH! WATCH, FORKED TONGUE!
SPLOOP!
GREAT! NOW IT'S TIME TO GO HOME, BROTHER FISH!
?
WHAT HAPPENED?
NOTHING. BUT YOU SHOULDN'T LET HIM WALK DOWN BY THE RIVER ON HIS OWN.
?
PALEFACE IS ALL WET. DID PALEFACE SAVE THE PAPOOSE FROM DROWNING?
SHUCKS, DON'T MENTION IT. IT WAS NOTHING, HONEST.
THE LIFE OF A PAPOOSE IS SACRED TO APACHES. PALEFACE HAS DONE WELL, EVEN IF HE DOESN'T WANT TO TALK ABOUT IT.
IF PALEFACE WISHES TO REMAIN IN THE TRIBE, HE MUST UNDERGO TESTS OF MANHOOD, JUST LIKE A REAL APACHE.
GET THE PALEFACE READY!
!

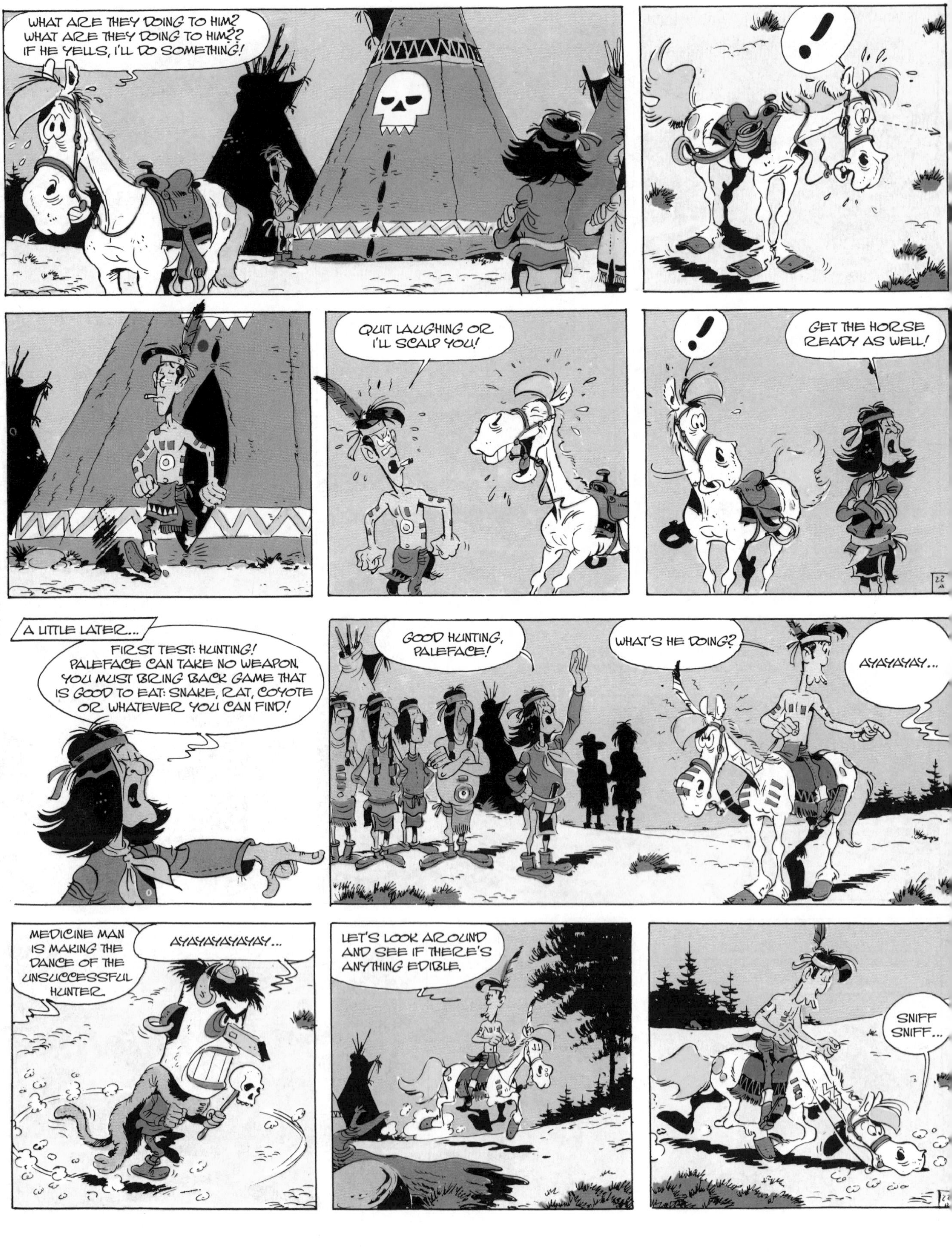

WHAT ARE THEY DOING TO HIM? WHAT ARE THEY DOING TO HIM?? IF HE YELLS, I'LL DO SOMETHING!
!
QUIT LAUGHING OR I'LL SCALP YOU!
!
GET THE HORSE READY AS WELL!
A LITTLE LATER...
FIRST TEST: HUNTING! PALEFACE CAN TAKE NO WEAPON. YOU MUST BRING BACK GAME THAT IS GOOD TO EAT: SNAKE, RAT, COYOTE OR WHATEVER YOU CAN FIND!
GOOD HUNTING, PALEFACE!
WHAT'S HE DOING?
AYAYAYAY...
MEDICINE MAN IS MAKING THE DANCE OF THE UNSUCCESSFUL HUNTER.
AYAYAYAYAYAY...
LET'S LOOK AROUND AND SEE IF THERE'S ANYTHING EDIBLE.
SNIFF SNIFF...

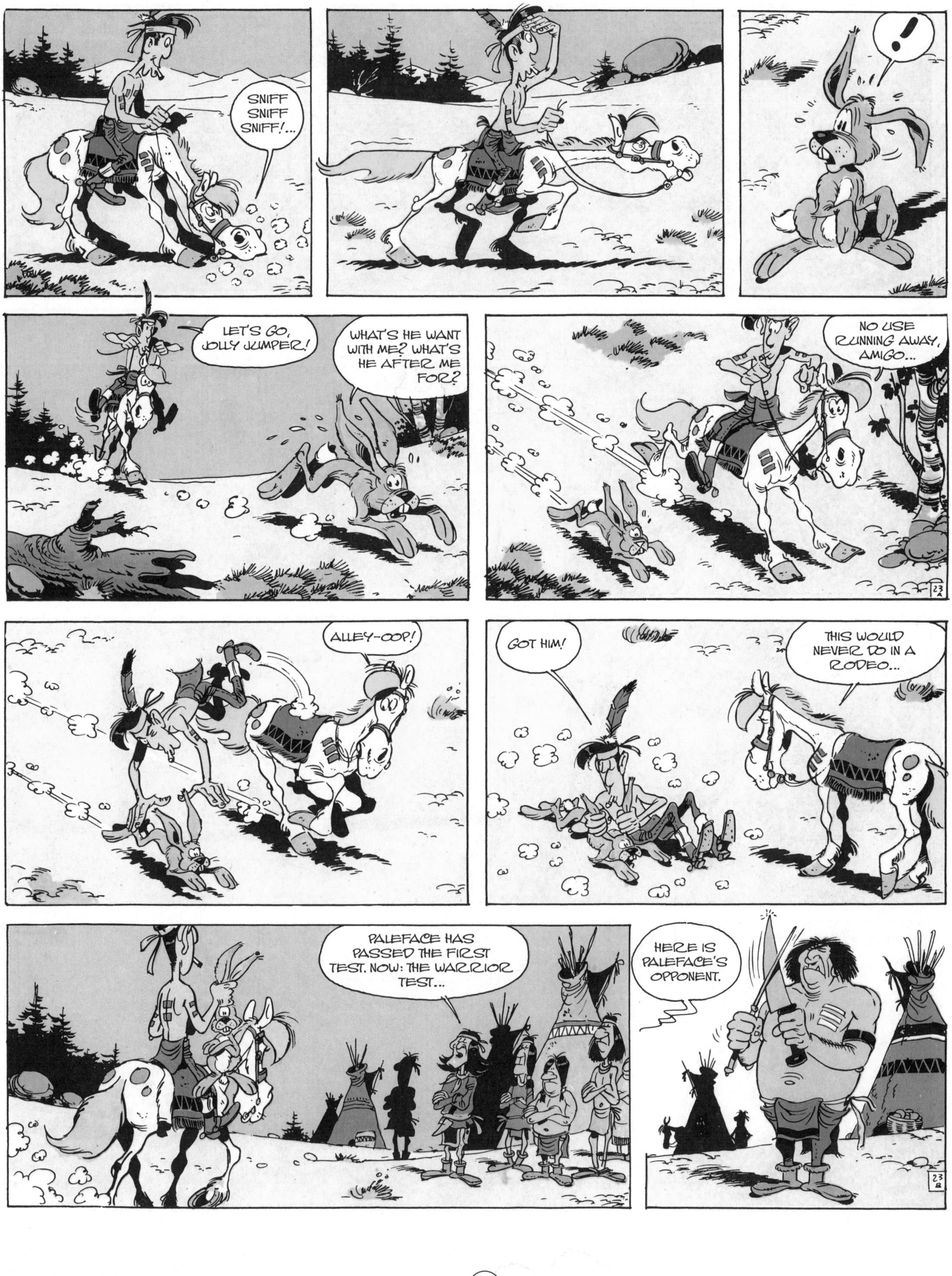
SNIFF SNIFF SNIFF!...
!
LET'S GO, JOLLY JUMPER!
WHAT'S HE WANT WITH ME? WHAT'S HE AFTER ME FOR?
NO USE RUNNING AWAY, AMIGO...
23 A
ALLEY-OOP!
GOT HIM!
THIS WOULD NEVER DO IN A RODEO...
PALEFACE HAS PASSED THE FIRST TEST. NOW: THE WARRIOR TEST...
HERE IS PALEFACE'S OPPONENT.
23 B

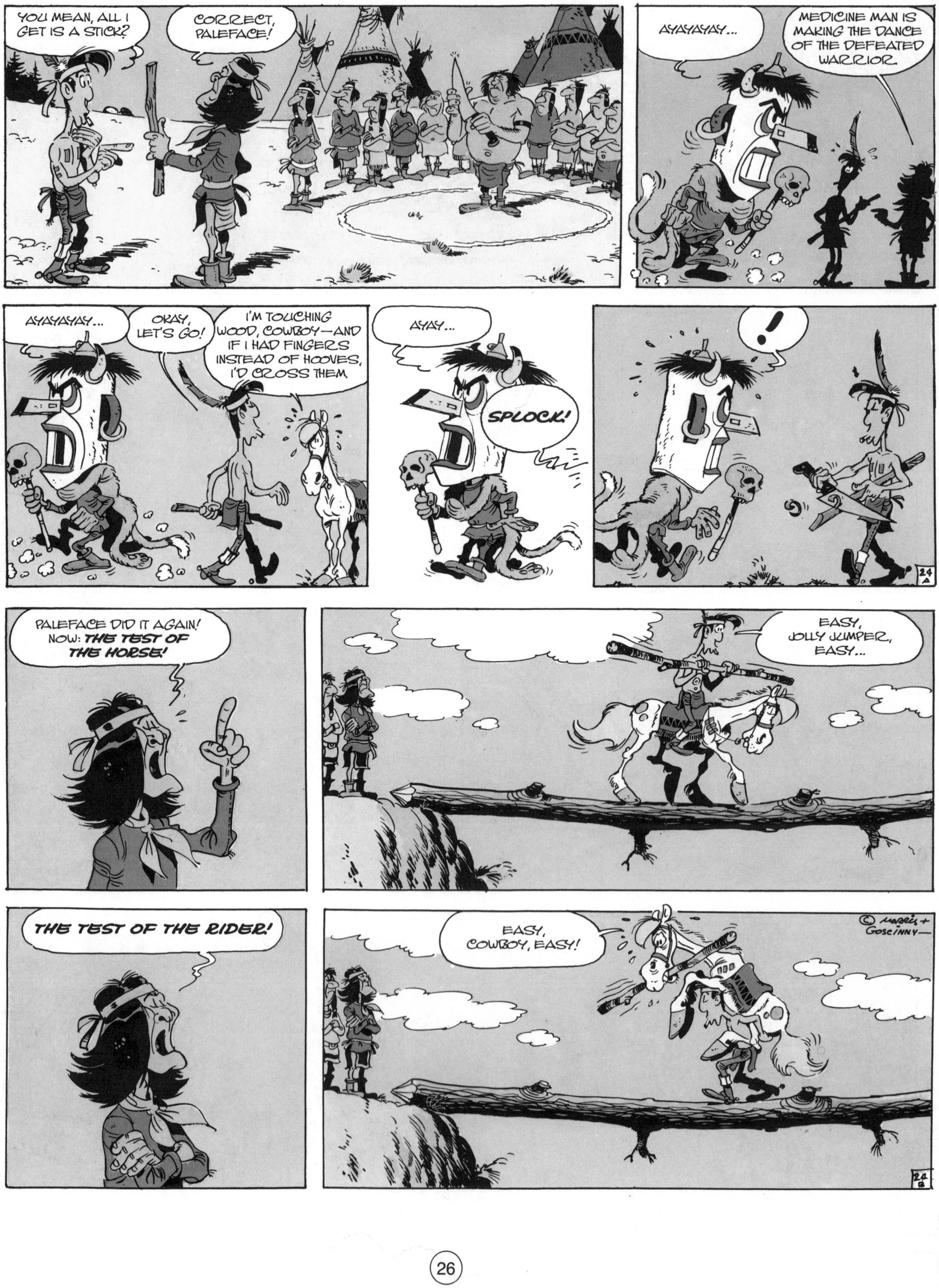
YOU MEAN, ALL I GET IS A STICK?
CORRECT, PALEFACE!
AYAYAYAY...
MEDICINE MAN IS MAKING THE DANCE OF THE DEFEATED WARRIOR.
AYAYAYAY...
OKAY, LET'S GO!
I'M TOUCHING WOOD, COWBOY—AND IF I HAD FINGERS INSTEAD OF HOOVES, I'D CROSS THEM.
AYAY...
SPLOCK!
!
PALEFACE DID IT AGAIN! NOW: THE TEST OF THE HORSE!
EASY, JOLLY JUMPER, EASY...
THE TEST OF THE RIDER!
EASY, COWBOY, EASY!
© MORRIS + GOSCINNY

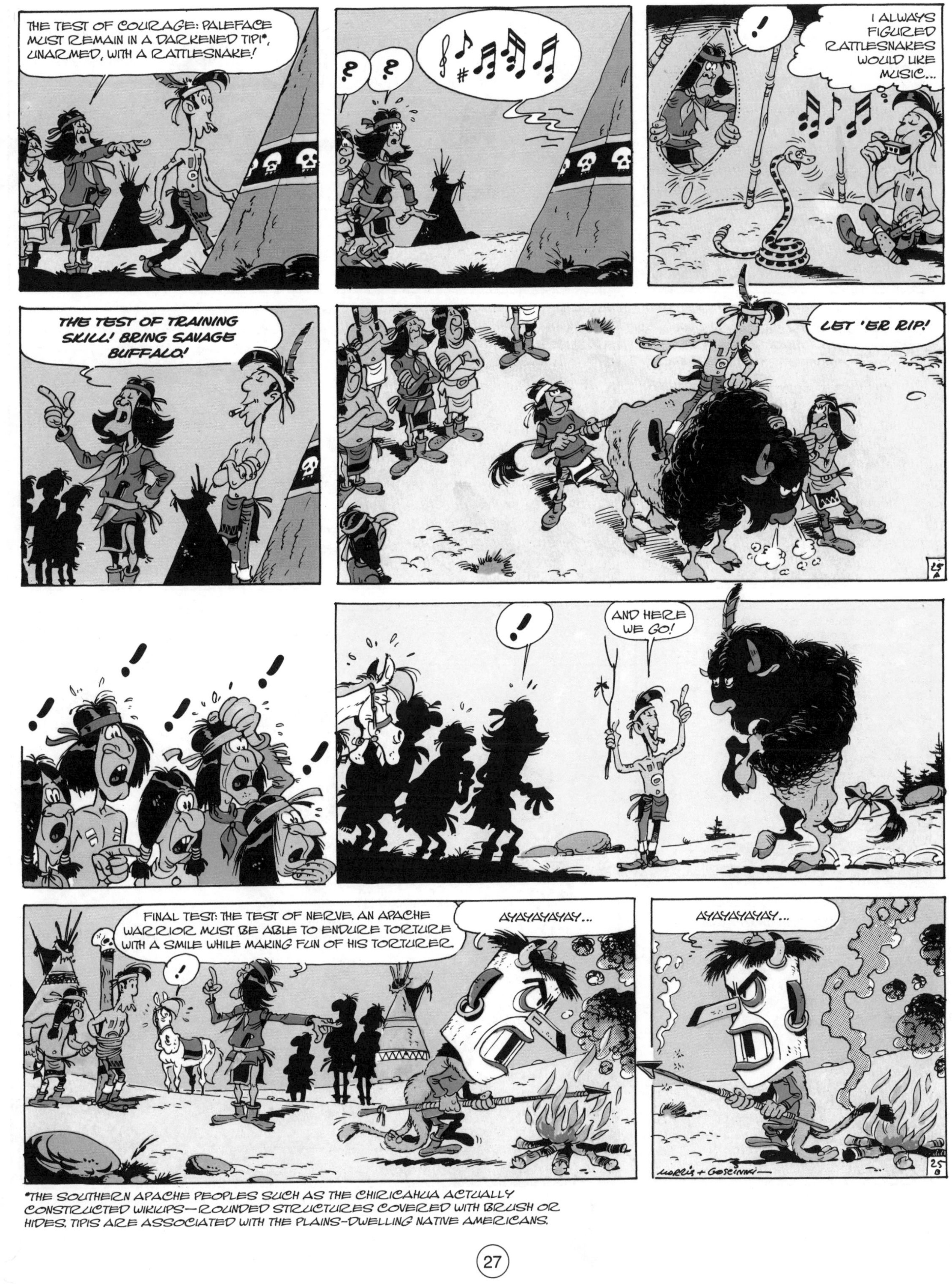
THE TEST OF COURAGE: PALEFACE MUST REMAIN IN A DARKENED TIPI*, UNARMED, WITH A RATTLESNAKE!
?
?
!
I ALWAYS FIGURED RATTLESNAKES WOULD LIKE MUSIC...
THE TEST OF TRAINING SKILL! BRING SAVAGE BUFFALO!
LET 'ER RIP!
!
AND HERE WE GO!
FINAL TEST: THE TEST OF NERVE. AN APACHE WARRIOR MUST BE ABLE TO ENDURE TORTURE WITH A SMILE WHILE MAKING FUN OF HIS TORTURER.
!
AYAYAYAYAY...
AYAYAYAYAY...

*THE SOUTHERN APACHE PEOPLES SUCH AS THE CHIRICAHUA ACTUALLY CONSTRUCTED WIKIUPS—ROUNDED STRUCTURES COVERED WITH BRUSH OR HIDES. TIPIS ARE ASSOCIATED WITH THE PLAINS-DWELLING NATIVE AMERICANS.

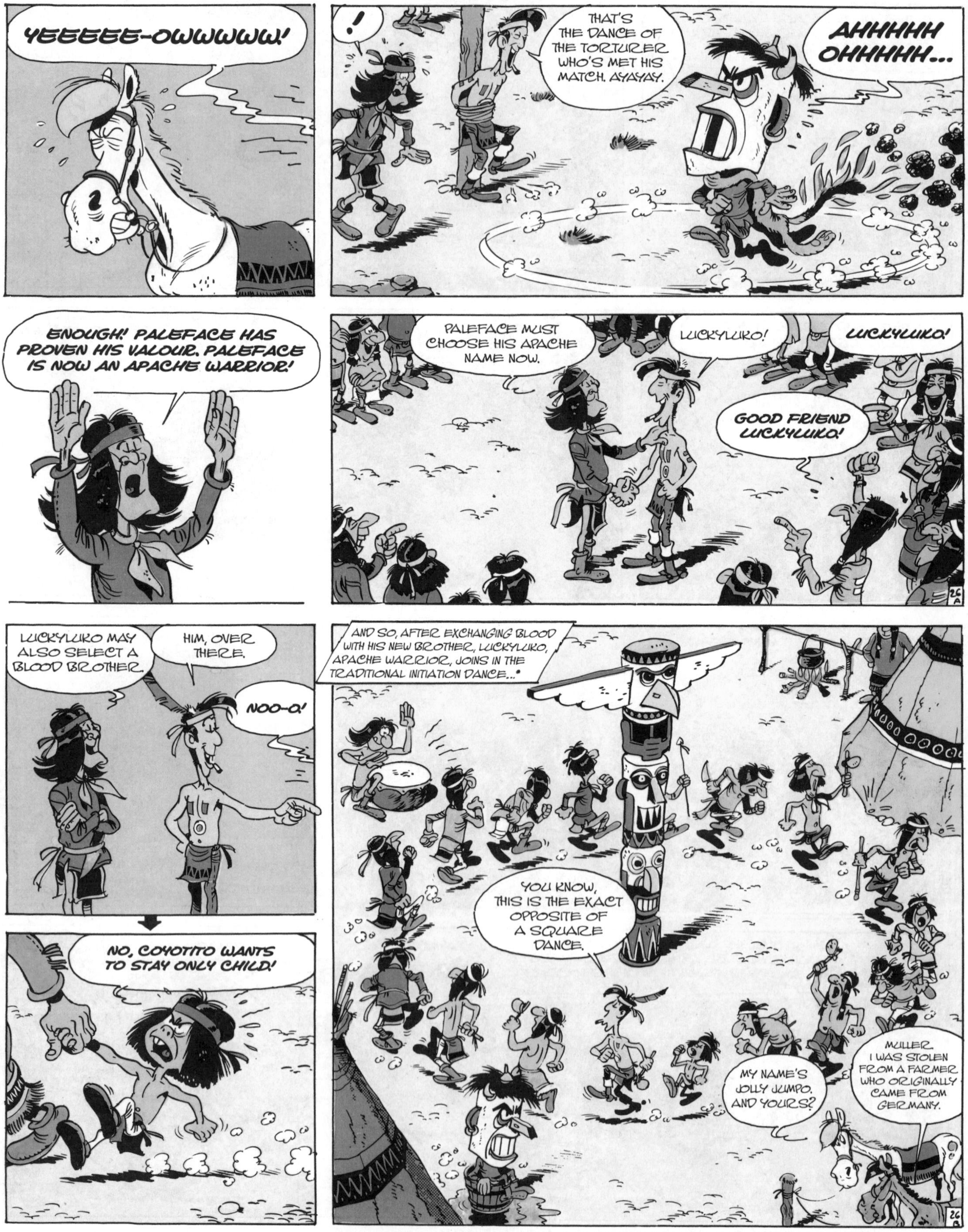

YEEEEE-OWWWWW!
!
THAT'S THE DANCE OF THE TORTURER WHO'S MET HIS MATCH. AYAYAY.
AHHHHH OHHHHH...
ENOUGH! PALEFACE HAS PROVEN HIS VALOUR. PALEFACE IS NOW AN APACHE WARRIOR!
PALEFACE MUST CHOOSE HIS APACHE NAME NOW.
LUCKYLUKO!
LUCKYLUKO!
GOOD FRIEND LUCKYLUKO!
26 A
LUCKYLUKO MAY ALSO SELECT A BLOOD BROTHER.
HIM, OVER THERE.
NOO-O!
NO, COYOTITO WANTS TO STAY ONLY CHILD!
AND SO, AFTER EXCHANGING BLOOD WITH HIS NEW BROTHER, LUCKYLUKO, APACHE WARRIOR, JOINS IN THE TRADITIONAL INITIATION DANCE...*
YOU KNOW, THIS IS THE EXACT OPPOSITE OF A SQUARE DANCE.
MY NAME'S JOLLY JUMPO. AND YOURS?
MULLER. I WAS STOLEN FROM A FARMER WHO ORIGINALLY CAME FROM GERMANY.
26 B

*AS A WORK OF FICTION, APACHE CANYON TAKES LIBERTIES WITH HISTORICAL ACCURACY. TOTEM POLES WERE COMMON TO SOME NORTHWEST NATIVE AMERICAN CULTURES, BUT NOT IN THE SOUTHWEST.

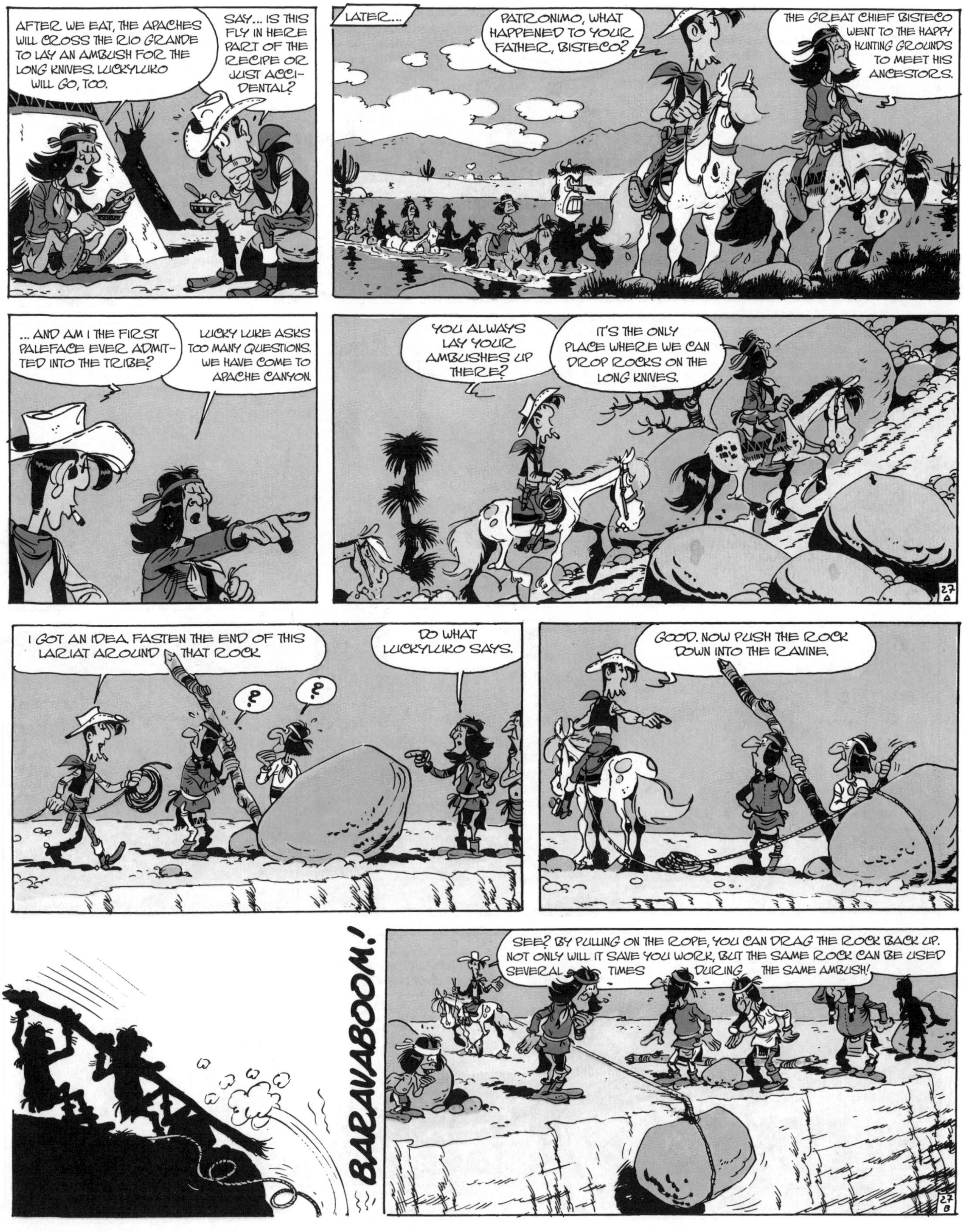

AFTER WE EAT, THE APACHES WILL CROSS THE RIO GRANDE TO LAY AN AMBUSH FOR THE LONG KNIVES. LUCKYLUKO WILL GO, TOO.
SAY... IS THIS FLY IN HERE PART OF THE RECIPE OR JUST ACCIDENTAL?
LATER...
PATRONIMO, WHAT HAPPENED TO YOUR FATHER, BISTECO?
THE GREAT CHIEF BISTECO WENT TO THE HAPPY HUNTING GROUNDS TO MEET HIS ANCESTORS.
... AND AM I THE FIRST PALEFACE EVER ADMITTED INTO THE TRIBE?
LUCKY LUKE ASKS TOO MANY QUESTIONS. WE HAVE COME TO APACHE CANYON.
YOU ALWAYS LAY YOUR AMBUSHES UP THERE?
IT'S THE ONLY PLACE WHERE WE CAN DROP ROCKS ON THE LONG KNIVES.
27 A
I GOT AN IDEA. FASTEN THE END OF THIS LARIAT AROUND THAT ROCK.
?
?
DO WHAT LUCKYLUKO SAYS.
GOOD. NOW PUSH THE ROCK DOWN INTO THE RAVINE.
BARAVABOOM!
SEE? BY PULLING ON THE ROPE, YOU CAN DRAG THE ROCK BACK UP. NOT ONLY WILL IT SAVE YOU WORK, BUT THE SAME ROCK CAN BE USED SEVERAL TIMES DURING THE SAME AMBUSH!
27 B

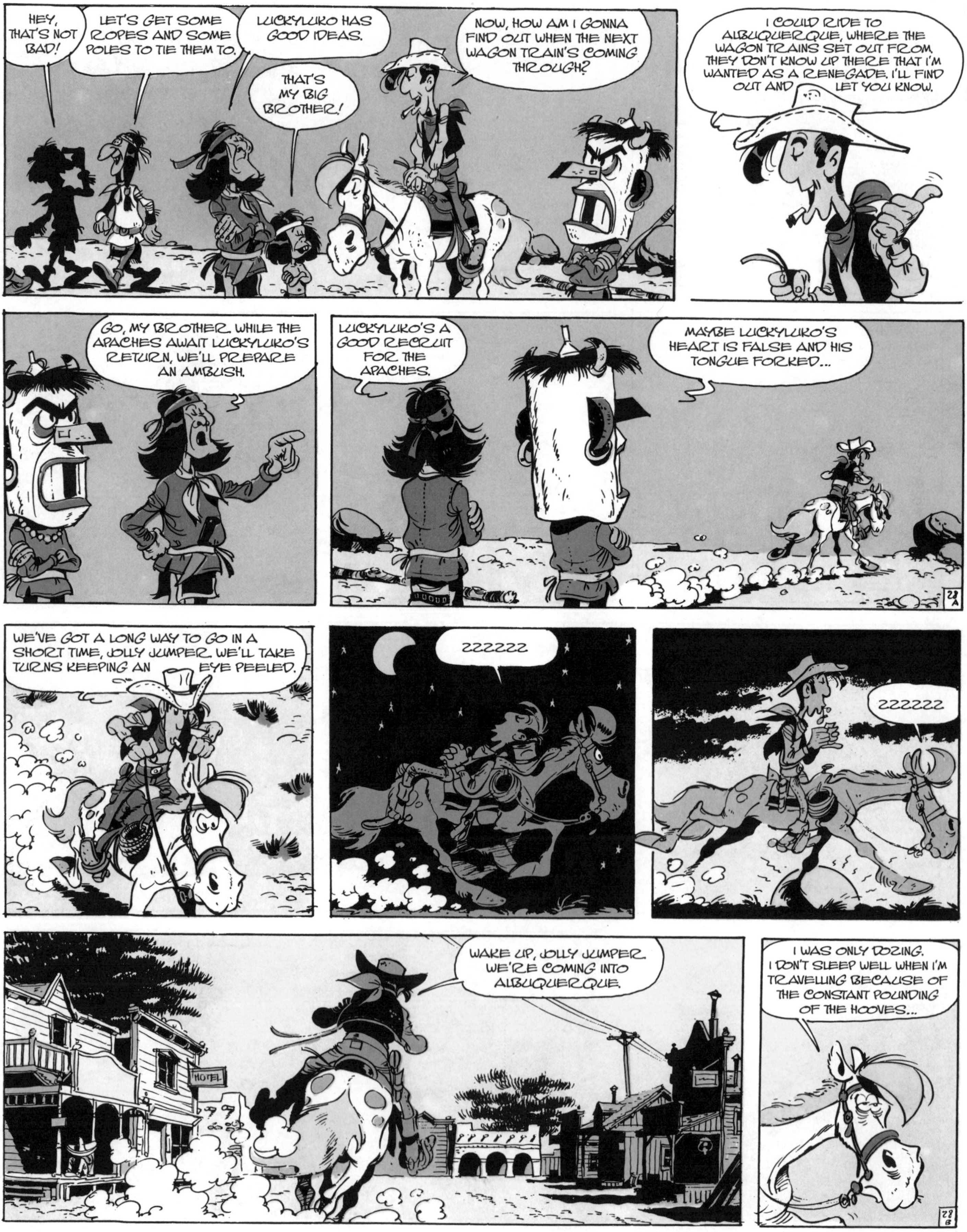
HEY, THAT'S NOT BAD!
LET'S GET SOME ROPES AND SOME POLES TO TIE THEM TO.
LUCKYLUKO HAS GOOD IDEAS.
THAT'S MY BIG BROTHER!
NOW, HOW AM I GONNA FIND OUT WHEN THE NEXT WAGON TRAIN'S COMING THROUGH?
I COULD RIDE TO ALBUQUERQUE, WHERE THE WAGON TRAINS SET OUT FROM. THEY DON'T KNOW UP THERE THAT I'M WANTED AS A RENEGADE. I'LL FIND OUT AND LET YOU KNOW.
GO, MY BROTHER. WHILE THE APACHES AWAIT LUCKYLUKO'S RETURN, WE'LL PREPARE AN AMBUSH.
LUCKYLUKO'S A GOOD RECRUIT FOR THE APACHES.
MAYBE LUCKYLUKO'S HEART IS FALSE AND HIS TONGUE FORKED...
28 A
WE'VE GOT A LONG WAY TO GO IN A SHORT TIME, JOLLY JUMPER. WE'LL TAKE TURNS KEEPING AN EYE PEELED.
ZZZZZZ
ZZZZZZ
HOTEL
WAKE UP, JOLLY JUMPER. WE'RE COMING INTO ALBUQUERQUE.
I WAS ONLY DOZING. I DON'T SLEEP WELL WHEN I'M TRAVELLING BECAUSE OF THE CONSTANT POUNDING OF THE HOOVES...
28 B

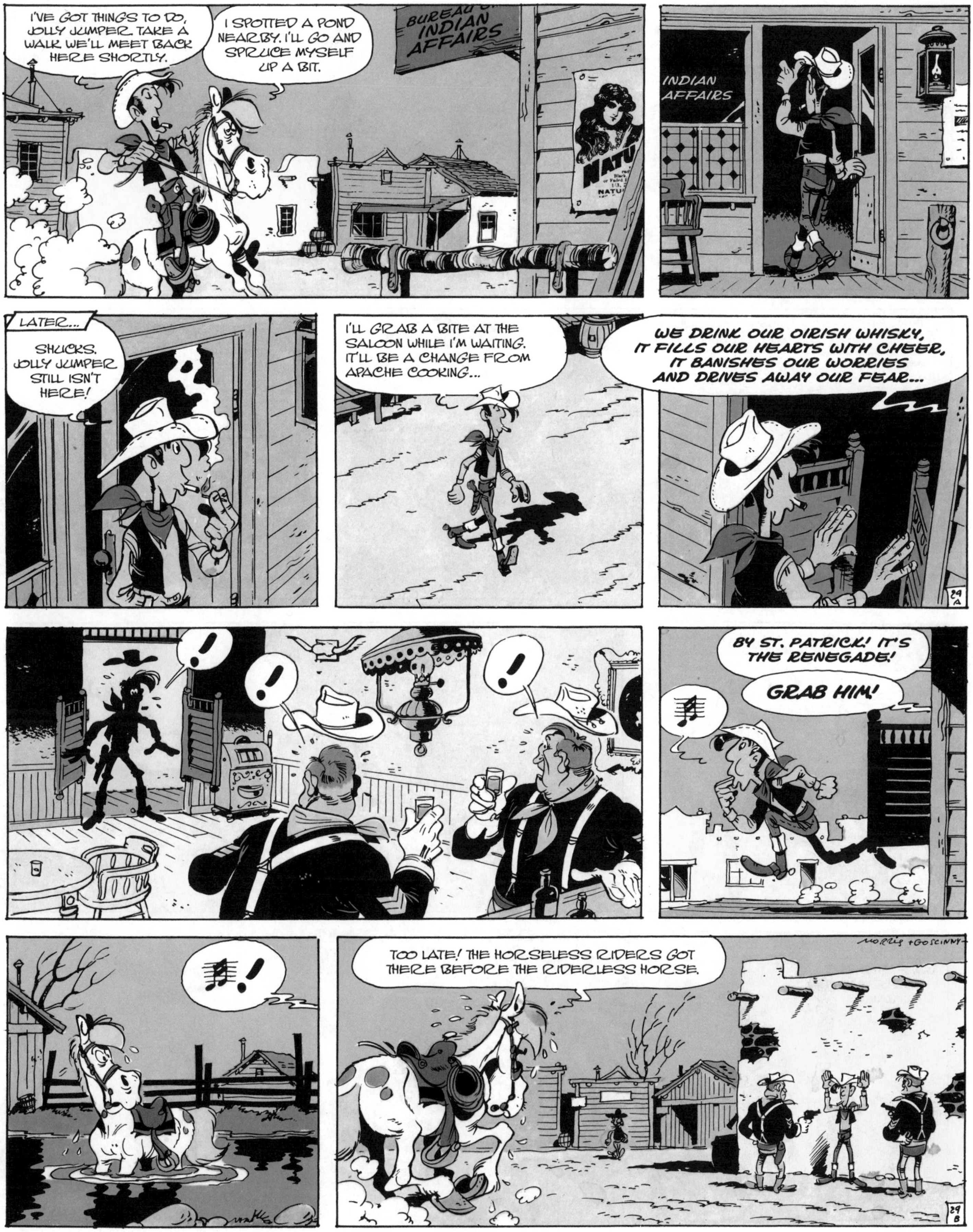
I'VE GOT THINGS TO DO, JOLLY JUMPER. TAKE A WALK. WE'LL MEET BACK HERE SHORTLY.
I SPOTTED A POND NEARBY. I'LL GO AND SPRUCE MYSELF UP A BIT.
INDIAN AFFAIRS
INDIAN AFFAIRS
LATER...
SHUCKS. JOLLY JUMPER STILL ISN'T HERE!
I'LL GRAB A BITE AT THE SALOON WHILE I'M WAITING. IT'LL BE A CHANGE FROM APACHE COOKING...
WE DRINK OUR OIRISH WHISKY, IT FILLS OUR HEARTS WITH CHEER, IT BANISHES OUR WORRIES AND DRIVES AWAY OUR FEAR...
29 A
!
!
!
BY ST. PATRICK! IT'S THE RENEGADE!
GRAB HIM!
MORRIS +GOSCINNY
!
TOO LATE! THE HORSELESS RIDERS GOT THERE BEFORE THE RIDERLESS HORSE.
29 B

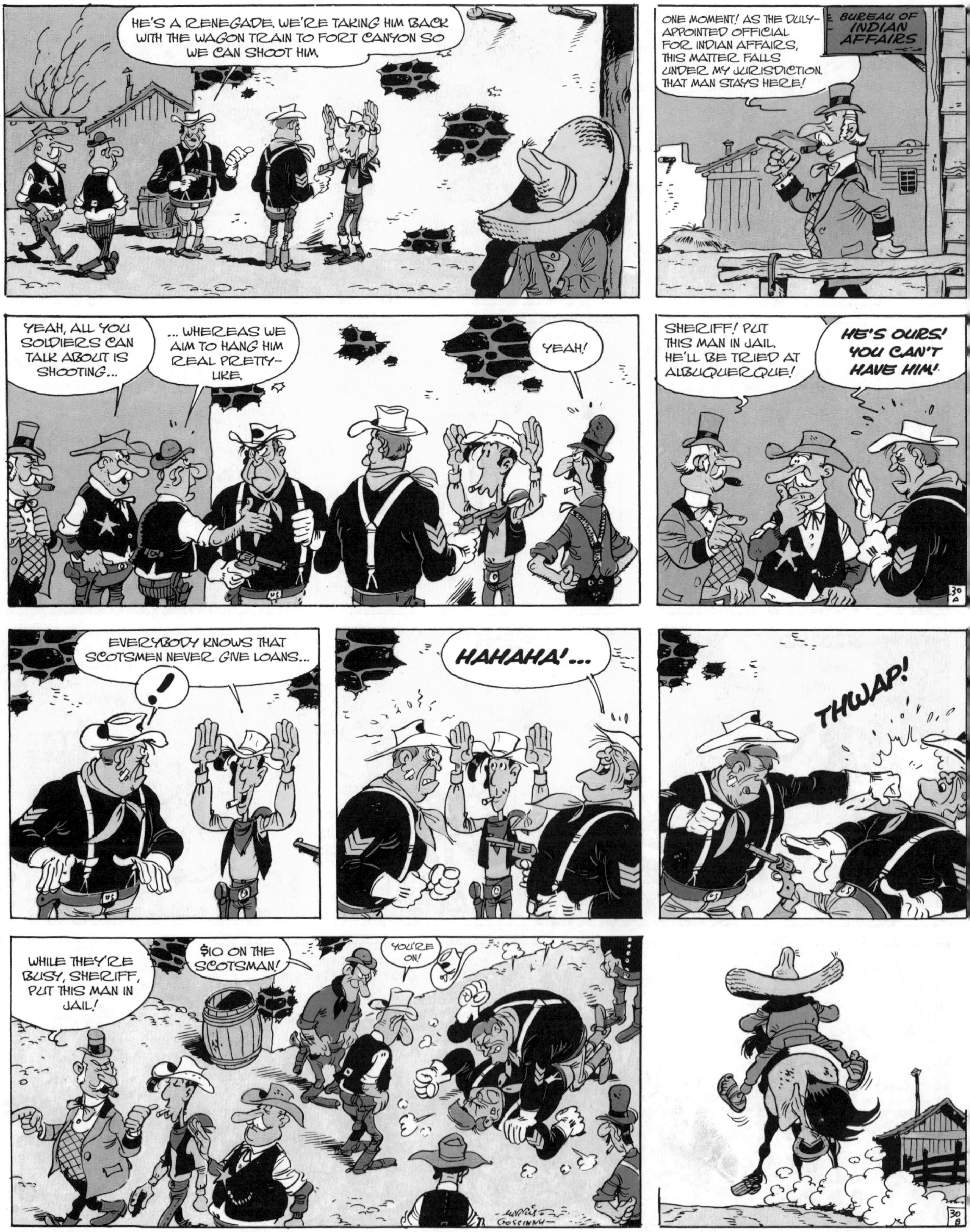
HE'S A RENEGADE. WE'RE TAKING HIM BACK WITH THE WAGON TRAIN TO FORT CANYON SO WE CAN SHOOT HIM.
ONE MOMENT! AS THE DULY-APPOINTED OFFICIAL FOR INDIAN AFFAIRS, THIS MATTER FALLS UNDER MY JURISDICTION. THAT MAN STAYS HERE!
BUREAU OF INDIAN AFFAIRS
YEAH, ALL YOU SOLDIERS CAN TALK ABOUT IS SHOOTING...
... WHEREAS WE AIM TO HANG HIM REAL PRETTY-LIKE.
YEAH!
SHERIFF! PUT THIS MAN IN JAIL. HE'LL BE TRIED AT ALBUQUERQUE!
HE'S OURS! YOU CAN'T HAVE HIM!
EVERYBODY KNOWS THAT SCOTSMEN NEVER GIVE LOANS...
!
HAHAHA!...
THWAP!
WHILE THEY'RE BUSY, SHERIFF, PUT THIS MAN IN JAIL!
$10 ON THE SCOTSMAN!
YOU'RE ON!
MORRIS GOSCINNY

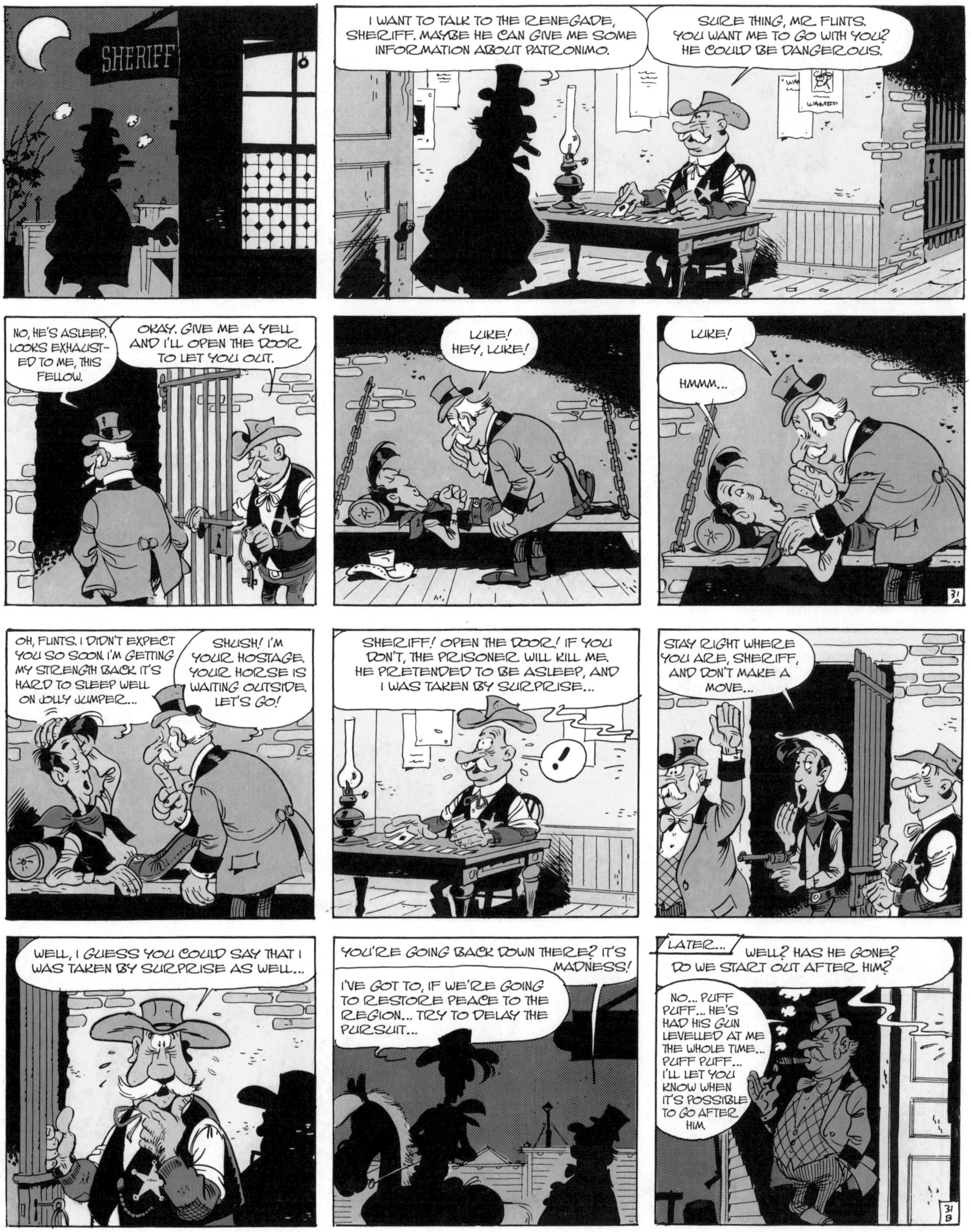
SHERIFF
I WANT TO TALK TO THE RENEGADE, SHERIFF. MAYBE HE CAN GIVE ME SOME INFORMATION ABOUT PATRONIMO.
SURE THING, MR. FLINTS. YOU WANT ME TO GO WITH YOU? HE COULD BE DANGEROUS.
NO, HE'S ASLEEP. LOOKS EXHAUSTED TO ME, THIS FELLOW.
OKAY. GIVE ME A YELL AND I'LL OPEN THE DOOR TO LET YOU OUT.
LUKE! HEY, LUKE!
LUKE!
HMMM...
OH, FLINTS. I DIDN'T EXPECT YOU SO SOON. I'M GETTING MY STRENGTH BACK. IT'S HARD TO SLEEP WELL ON JOLLY JUMPER...
SHUSH! I'M YOUR HOSTAGE. YOUR HORSE IS WAITING OUTSIDE. LET'S GO!
SHERIFF! OPEN THE DOOR! IF YOU DON'T, THE PRISONER WILL KILL ME. HE PRETENDED TO BE ASLEEP, AND I WAS TAKEN BY SURPRISE...
!
STAY RIGHT WHERE YOU ARE, SHERIFF, AND DON'T MAKE A MOVE...
WELL, I GUESS YOU COULD SAY THAT I WAS TAKEN BY SURPRISE AS WELL...
YOU'RE GOING BACK DOWN THERE? IT'S MADNESS!
I'VE GOT TO, IF WE'RE GOING TO RESTORE PEACE TO THE REGION... TRY TO DELAY THE PURSUIT...
LATER...
WELL? HAS HE GONE? DO WE START OUT AFTER HIM?
NO... PUFF PUFF... HE'S HAD HIS GUN LEVELLED AT ME THE WHOLE TIME... PUFF PUFF... I'LL LET YOU KNOW WHEN IT'S POSSIBLE TO GO AFTER HIM.

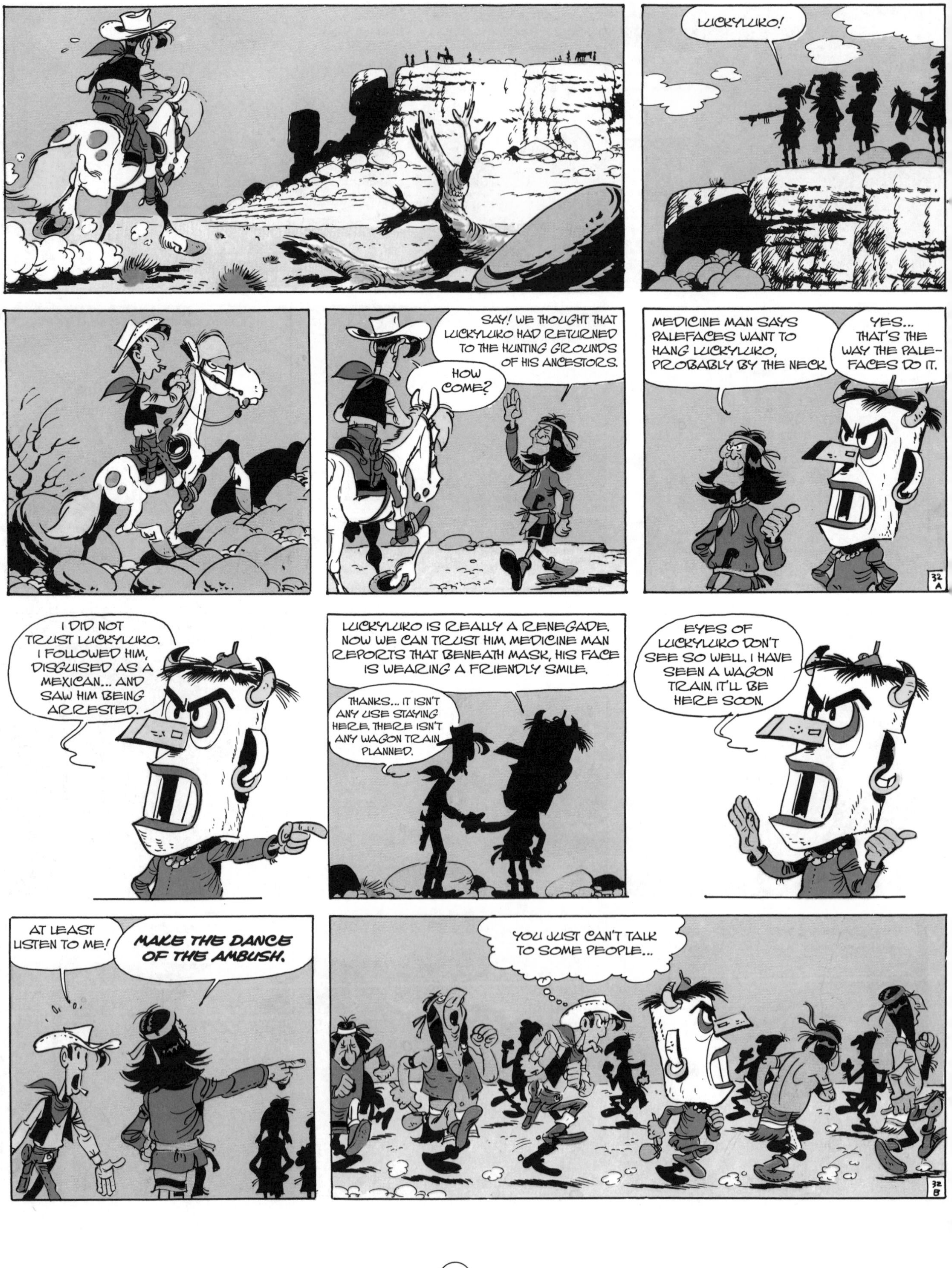

LUCKYLUKO!
SAY! WE THOUGHT THAT LUCKYLUKO HAD RETURNED TO THE HUNTING GROUNDS OF HIS ANCESTORS.
HOW COME?
MEDICINE MAN SAYS PALEFACES WANT TO HANG LUCKYLUKO, PROBABLY BY THE NECK.
YES... THAT'S THE WAY THE PALE-FACES DO IT.
I DID NOT TRUST LUCKYLUKO. I FOLLOWED HIM, DISGUISED AS A MEXICAN... AND SAW HIM BEING ARRESTED.
LUCKYLUKO IS REALLY A RENEGADE. NOW WE CAN TRUST HIM. MEDICINE MAN REPORTS THAT BENEATH MASK, HIS FACE IS WEARING A FRIENDLY SMILE.
THANKS... IT ISN'T ANY USE STAYING HERE. THERE ISN'T ANY WAGON TRAIN PLANNED.
EYES OF LUCKYLUKO DON'T SEE SO WELL. I HAVE SEEN A WAGON TRAIN. IT'LL BE HERE SOON.
AT LEAST LISTEN TO ME!
MAKE THE DANCE OF THE AMBUSH.
YOU JUST CAN'T TALK TO SOME PEOPLE...

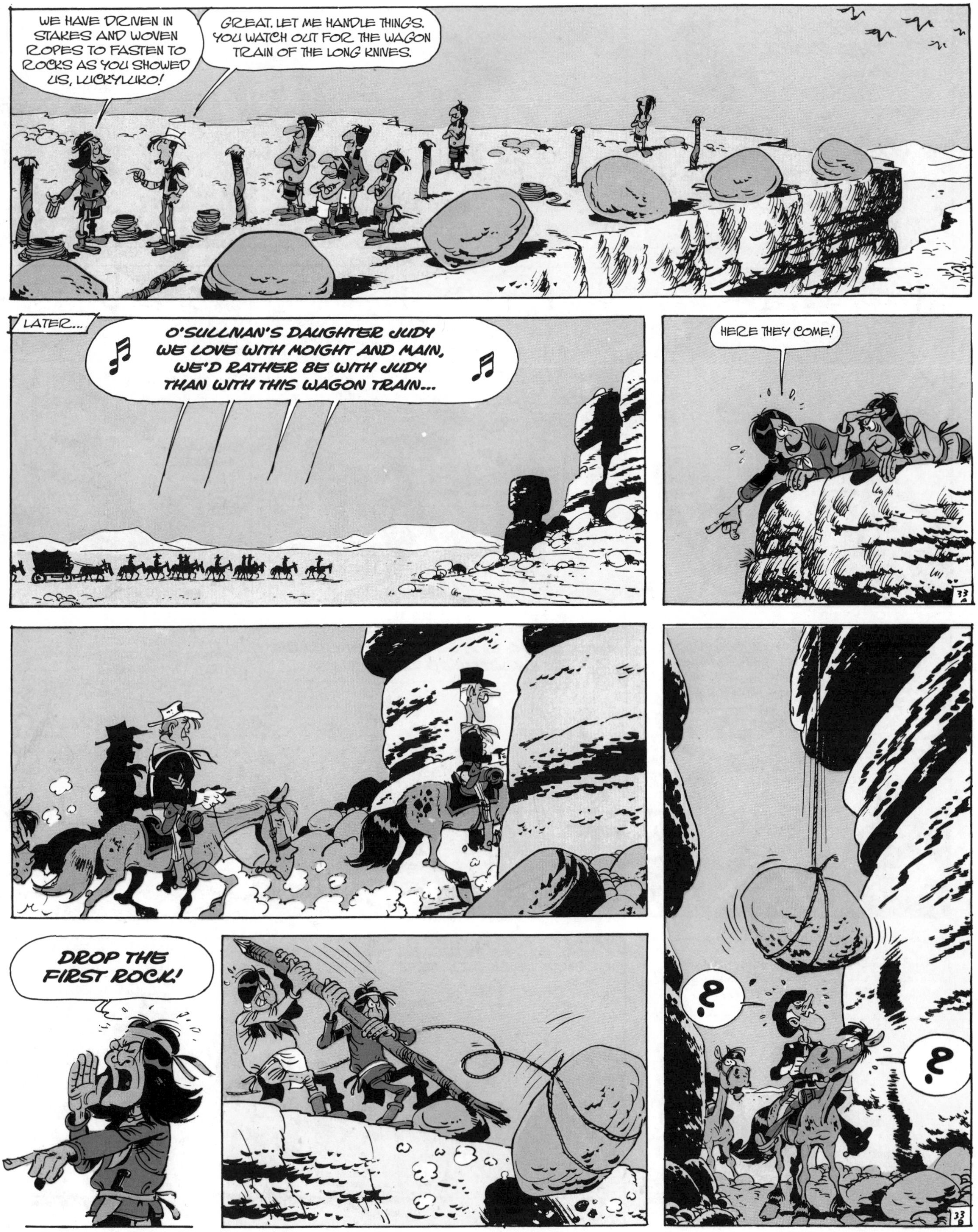

WE HAVE DRIVEN IN STAKES AND WOVEN ROPES TO FASTEN TO ROCKS AS YOU SHOWED US, LUCKYLUKO!
GREAT. LET ME HANDLE THINGS. YOU WATCH OUT FOR THE WAGON TRAIN OF THE LONG KNIVES.
LATER...
O'SULLIVAN'S DAUGHTER JUDY WE LOVE WITH MOIGHT AND MAIN, WE'D RATHER BE WITH JUDY THAN WITH THIS WAGON TRAIN...
HERE THEY COME!
DROP THE FIRST ROCK!
?
?

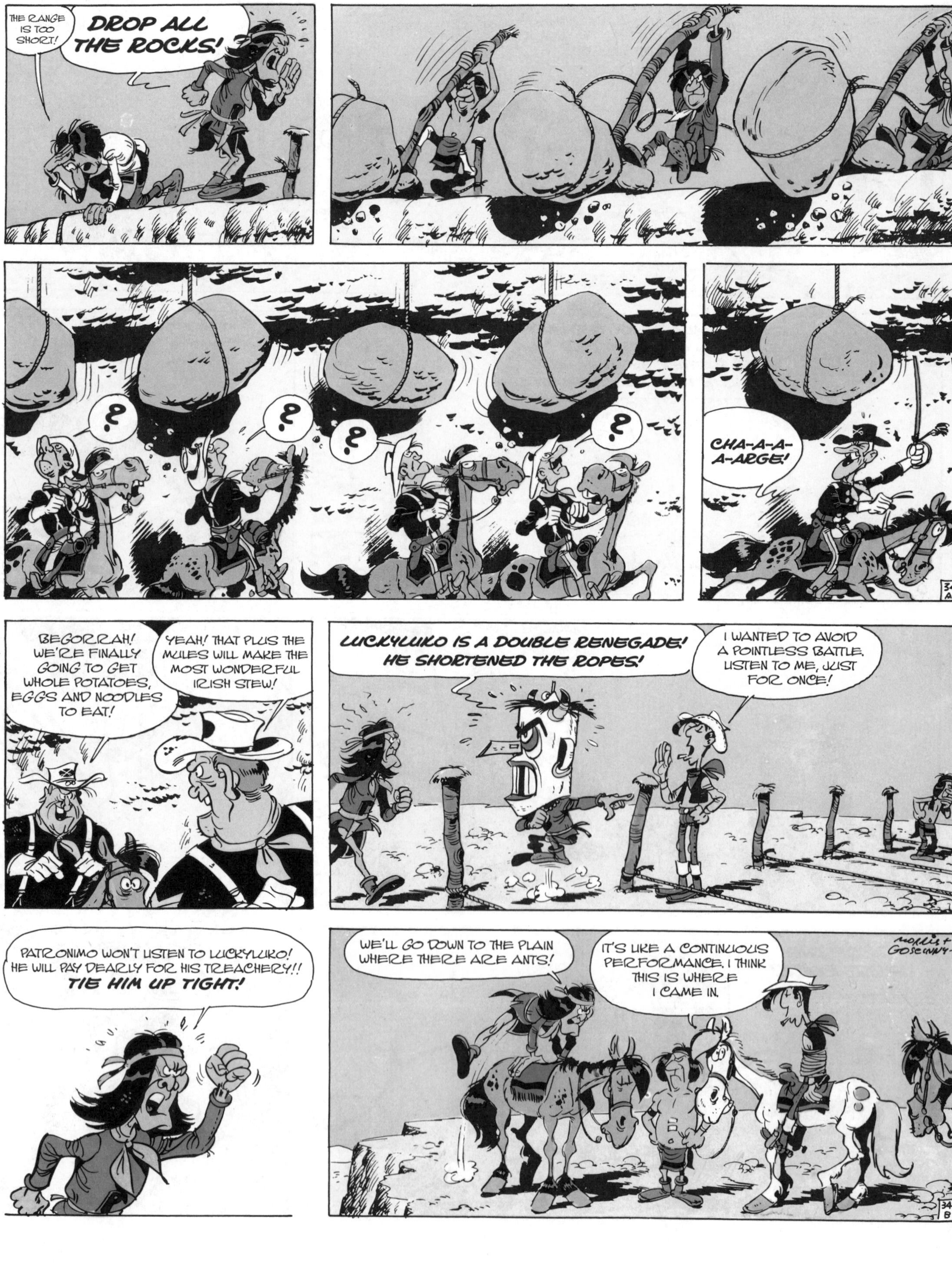
THE RANGE IS TOO SHORT!
DROP ALL THE ROCKS!
?
?
?
?
CHA-A-A-A-ARGE!
BEGORRAH! WE'RE FINALLY GOING TO GET WHOLE POTATOES, EGGS AND NOODLES TO EAT!
YEAH! THAT PLUS THE MULES WILL MAKE THE MOST WONDERFUL IRISH STEW!
LUCKYLUKO IS A DOUBLE RENEGADE! HE SHORTENED THE ROPES!
I WANTED TO AVOID A POINTLESS BATTLE. LISTEN TO ME, JUST FOR ONCE!
PATRONIMO WON'T LISTEN TO LUCKYLUKO! HE WILL PAY DEARLY FOR HIS TREACHERY!! TIE HIM UP TIGHT!
WE'LL GO DOWN TO THE PLAIN WHERE THERE ARE ANTS!
IT'S LIKE A CONTINUOUS PERFORMANCE. I THINK THIS IS WHERE I CAME IN.

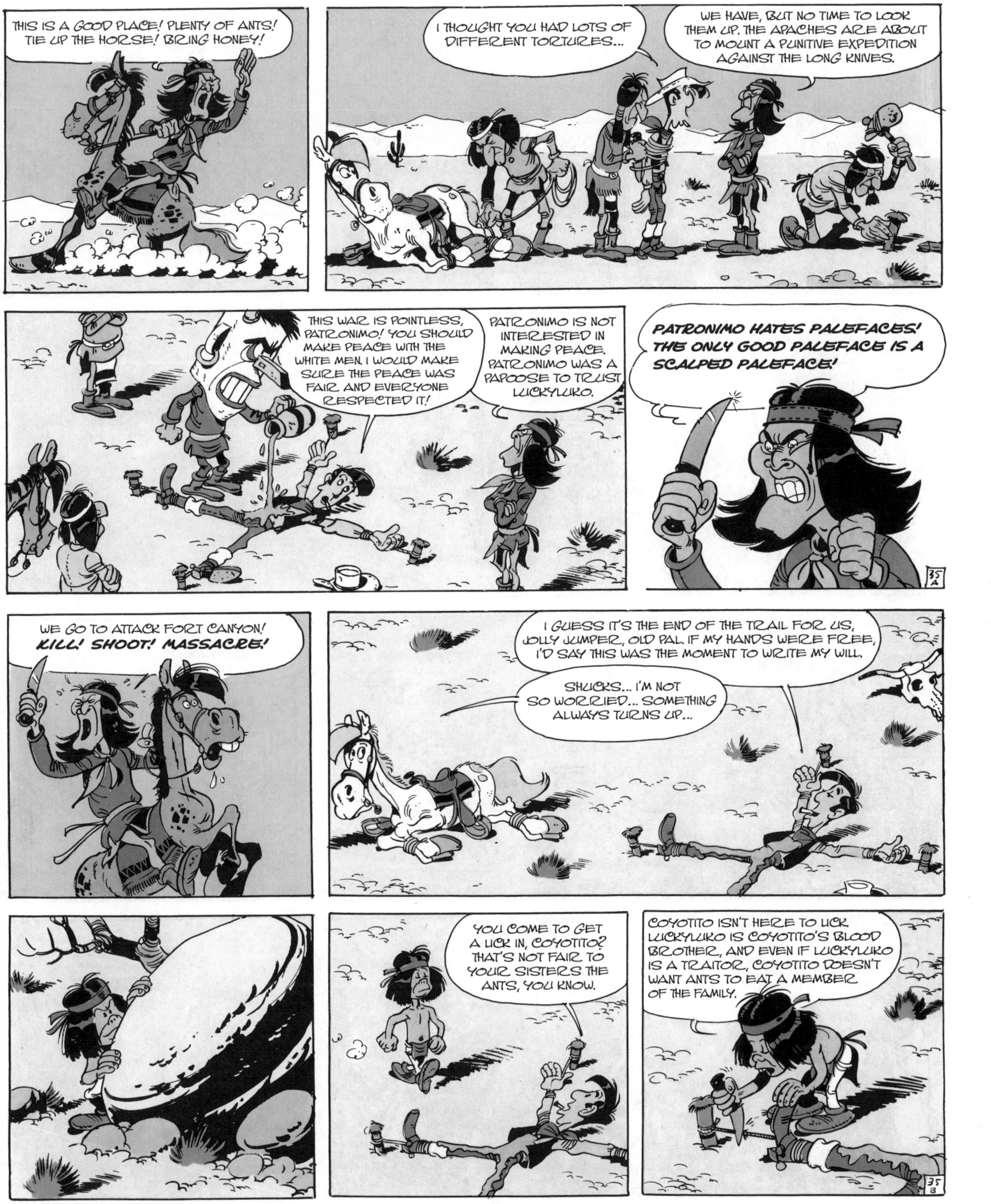

THIS IS A GOOD PLACE! PLENTY OF ANTS! TIE UP THE HORSE! BRING HONEY!
I THOUGHT YOU HAD LOTS OF DIFFERENT TORTURES...
WE HAVE, BUT NO TIME TO LOOK THEM UP. THE APACHES ARE ABOUT TO MOUNT A PUNITIVE EXPEDITION AGAINST THE LONG KNIVES.
THIS WAR IS POINTLESS, PATRONIMO! YOU SHOULD MAKE PEACE WITH THE WHITE MEN. I WOULD MAKE SURE THE PEACE WAS FAIR AND EVERYONE RESPECTED IT!
PATRONIMO IS NOT INTERESTED IN MAKING PEACE. PATRONIMO WAS A PAPOOSE TO TRUST LUCKYLUKO.
PATRONIMO HATES PALEFACES! THE ONLY GOOD PALEFACE IS A SCALPED PALEFACE!
35 A
WE GO TO ATTACK FORT CANYON! KILL! SHOOT! MASSACRE!
I GUESS IT'S THE END OF THE TRAIL FOR US, JOLLY JUMPER, OLD PAL. IF MY HANDS WERE FREE, I'D SAY THIS WAS THE MOMENT TO WRITE MY WILL.
SHUCKS... I'M NOT SO WORRIED... SOMETHING ALWAYS TURNS UP...
YOU COME TO GET A LICK IN, COYOTITO? THAT'S NOT FAIR TO YOUR SISTERS THE ANTS, YOU KNOW.
COYOTITO ISN'T HERE TO LICK. LUCKYLUKO IS COYOTITO'S BLOOD BROTHER, AND EVEN IF LUCKYLUKO IS A TRAITOR, COYOTITO DOESN'T WANT ANTS TO EAT A MEMBER OF THE FAMILY.
35 B

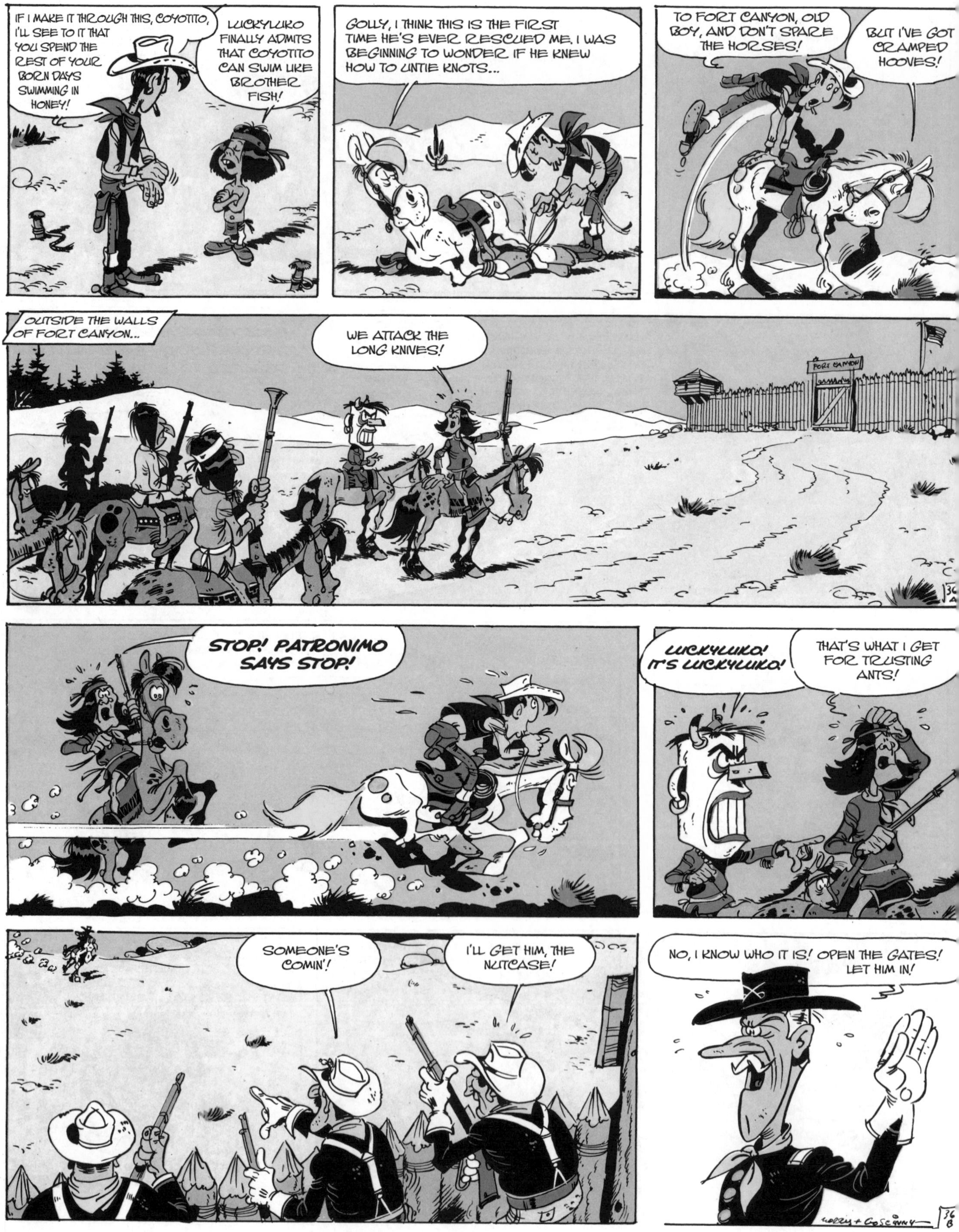

IF I MAKE IT THROUGH THIS, COYOTITO, I'LL SEE TO IT THAT YOU SPEND THE REST OF YOUR BORN DAYS SWIMMING IN HONEY!
LUCKYLUKO FINALLY ADMITS THAT COYOTITO CAN SWIM LIKE BROTHER FISH!
GOLLY, I THINK THIS IS THE FIRST TIME HE'S EVER RESCUED ME. I WAS BEGINNING TO WONDER IF HE KNEW HOW TO UNTIE KNOTS...
TO FORT CANYON, OLD BOY, AND DON'T SPARE THE HORSES!
BUT I'VE GOT CRAMPED HOOVES!
OUTSIDE THE WALLS OF FORT CANYON...
WE ATTACK THE LONG KNIVES!
STOP! PATRONIMO SAYS STOP!
LUCKYLUKO! IT'S LUCKYLUKO!
THAT'S WHAT I GET FOR TRUSTING ANTS!
SOMEONE'S COMIN'!
I'LL GET HIM, THE NUTCASE!
NO, I KNOW WHO IT IS! OPEN THE GATES! LET HIM IN!

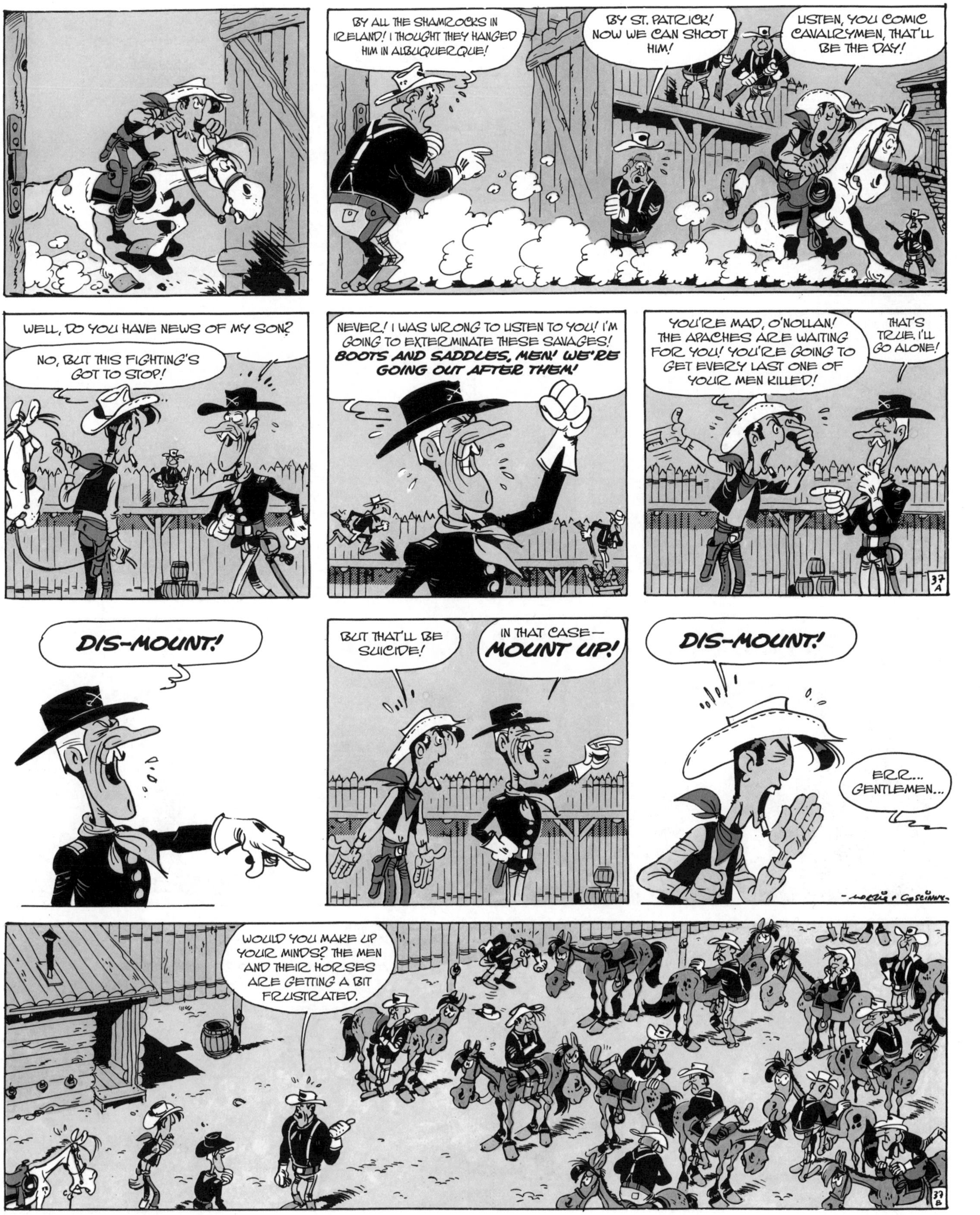
BY ALL THE SHAMROCKS IN IRELAND! I THOUGHT THEY HANGED HIM IN ALBUQUERQUE!
BY ST. PATRICK! NOW WE CAN SHOOT HIM!
LISTEN, YOU COMIC CAVALRYMEN, THAT'LL BE THE DAY!
WELL, DO YOU HAVE NEWS OF MY SON?
NO, BUT THIS FIGHTING'S GOT TO STOP!
NEVER! I WAS WRONG TO LISTEN TO YOU! I'M GOING TO EXTERMINATE THESE SAVAGES! BOOTS AND SADDLES, MEN! WE'RE GOING OUT AFTER THEM!
YOU'RE MAD, O'NOLLAN! THE APACHES ARE WAITING FOR YOU! YOU'RE GOING TO GET EVERY LAST ONE OF YOUR MEN KILLED!
THAT'S TRUE. I'LL GO ALONE!
37 A
DIS-MOUNT!
BUT THAT'LL BE SUICIDE!
IN THAT CASE— MOUNT UP!
DIS-MOUNT!
ERR... GENTLEMEN...
WOULD YOU MAKE UP YOUR MINDS? THE MEN AND THEIR HORSES ARE GETTING A BIT FRUSTRATED.
37 B

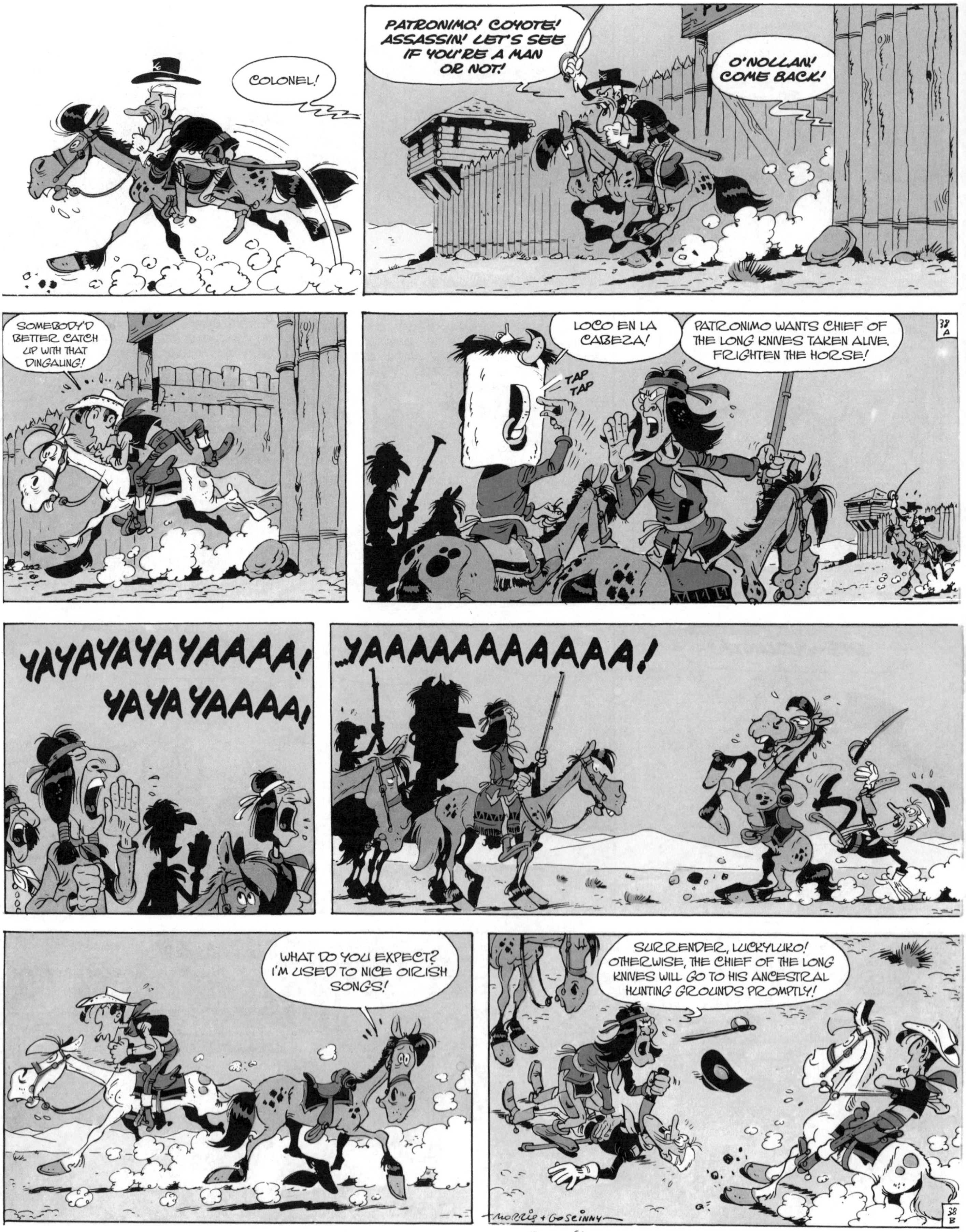
COLONEL!
PATRONIMO! COYOTE! ASSASSIN! LET'S SEE IF YOU'RE A MAN OR NOT!
O'NOLLAN! COME BACK!
SOMEBODY'D BETTER CATCH UP WITH THAT DINGALING!
LOCO EN LA CABEZA!
TAP TAP
PATRONIMO WANTS CHIEF OF THE LONG KNIVES TAKEN ALIVE. FRIGHTEN THE HORSE!
38 A
YAYAYAYAYAAAAA! YAYA YAAAA!
...YAAAAAAAAAAA!
WHAT DO YOU EXPECT? I'M USED TO NICE OIRISH SONGS!
SURRENDER, LUCKYLUKO! OTHERWISE, THE CHIEF OF THE LONG KNIVES WILL GO TO HIS ANCESTRAL HUNTING GROUNDS PROMPTLY!
MORRIS + GOSCINNY
38 B

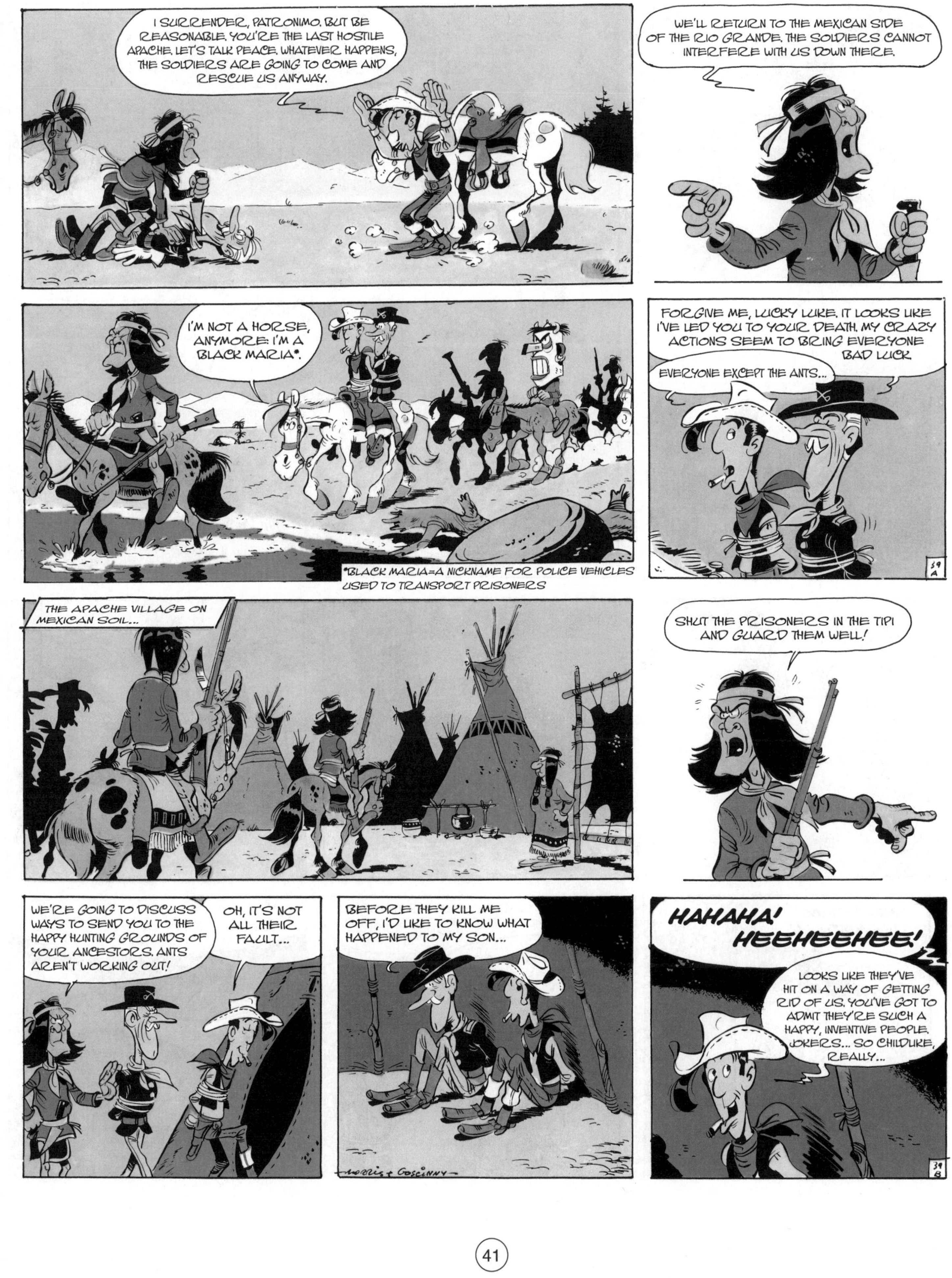
I SURRENDER, PATRONIMO. BUT BE REASONABLE. YOU'RE THE LAST HOSTILE APACHE. LET'S TALK PEACE. WHATEVER HAPPENS, THE SOLDIERS ARE GOING TO COME AND RESCUE US ANYWAY.
WE'LL RETURN TO THE MEXICAN SIDE OF THE RIO GRANDE. THE SOLDIERS CANNOT INTERFERE WITH US DOWN THERE.
I'M NOT A HORSE, ANYMORE: I'M A BLACK MARIA*.
*BLACK MARIA=A NICKNAME FOR POLICE VEHICLES USED TO TRANSPORT PRISONERS
FORGIVE ME, LUCKY LUKE. IT LOOKS LIKE I'VE LED YOU TO YOUR DEATH. MY CRAZY ACTIONS SEEM TO BRING EVERYONE BAD LUCK.
EVERYONE EXCEPT THE ANTS...
THE APACHE VILLAGE ON MEXICAN SOIL...
SHUT THE PRISONERS IN THE TIPI AND GUARD THEM WELL!
WE'RE GOING TO DISCUSS WAYS TO SEND YOU TO THE HAPPY HUNTING GROUNDS OF YOUR ANCESTORS. ANTS AREN'T WORKING OUT!
OH, IT'S NOT ALL THEIR FAULT...
BEFORE THEY KILL ME OFF, I'D LIKE TO KNOW WHAT HAPPENED TO MY SON...
MORRIS + GOSCINNY
HAHAHA! HEEHEEHEE!
LOOKS LIKE THEY'VE HIT ON A WAY OF GETTING RID OF US. YOU'VE GOT TO ADMIT THEY'RE SUCH A HAPPY, INVENTIVE PEOPLE. JOKERS... SO CHILDLIKE, REALLY...

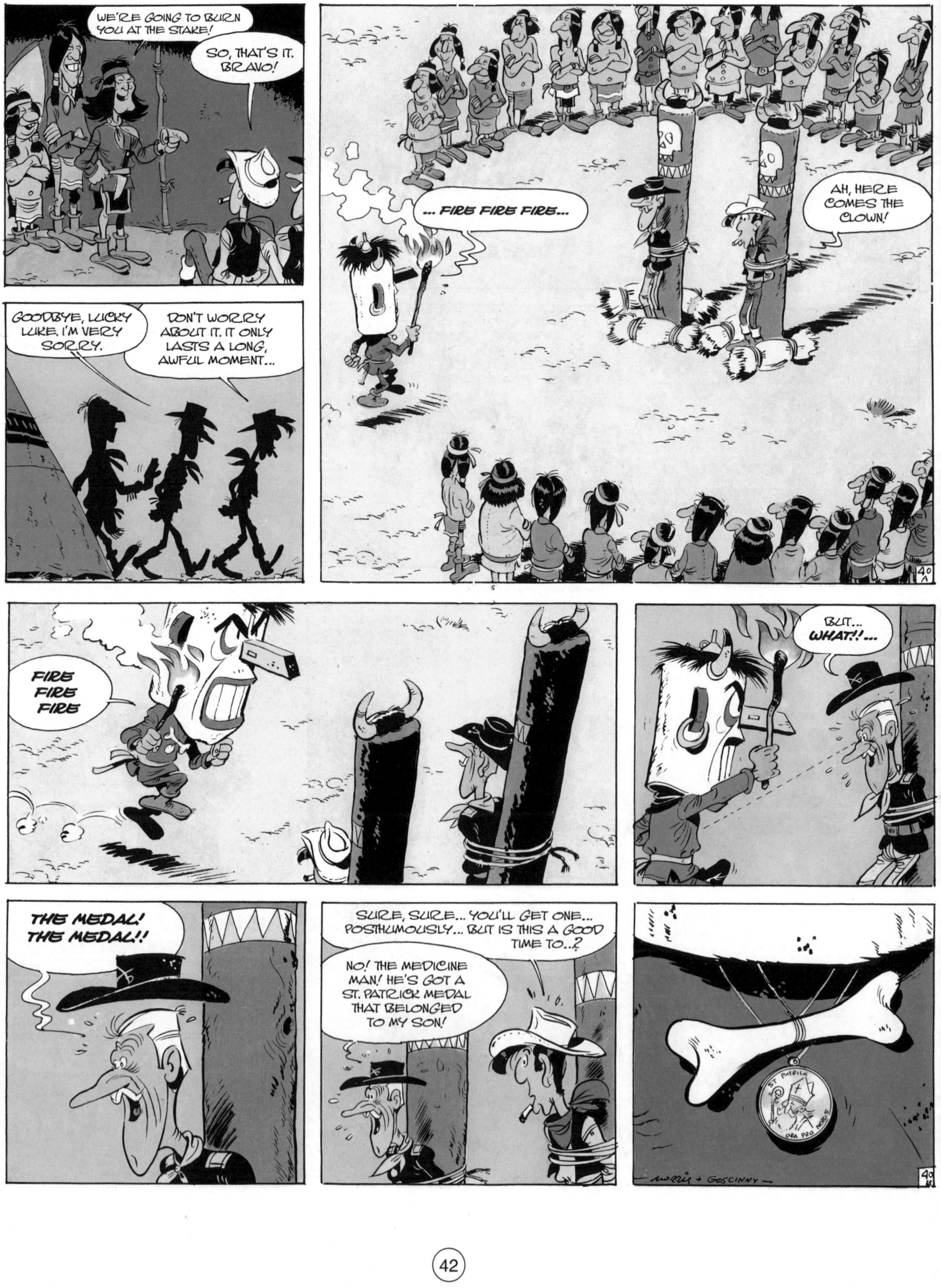
WE'RE GOING TO BURN YOU AT THE STAKE!
SO, THAT'S IT. BRAVO!
GOODBYE, LUCKY LUKE. I'M VERY SORRY.
DON'T WORRY ABOUT IT. IT ONLY LASTS A LONG, AWFUL MOMENT...
... FIRE FIRE FIRE...
AH, HERE COMES THE CLOWN!
FIRE FIRE FIRE
BUT... WHAT!!...
THE MEDAL! THE MEDAL!!
SURE, SURE... YOU'LL GET ONE... POSTHUMOUSLY... BUT IS THIS A GOOD TIME TO...?
NO! THE MEDICINE MAN! HE'S GOT A ST. PATRICK MEDAL THAT BELONGED TO MY SON!
ST PATRICK
ORA PRO NOBIS

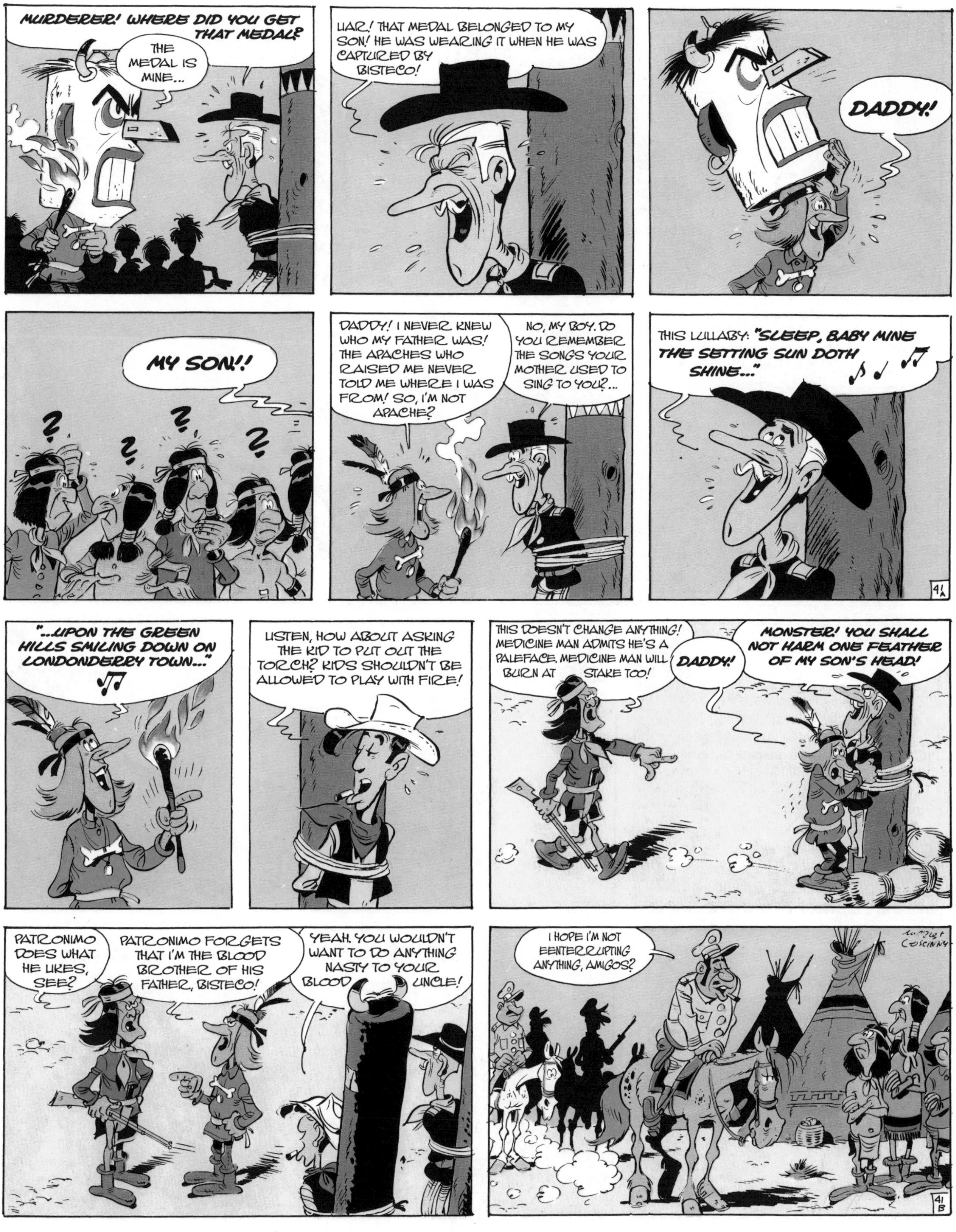
MURDERER! WHERE DID YOU GET THAT MEDAL?
THE MEDAL IS MINE...
LIAR! THAT MEDAL BELONGED TO MY SON! HE WAS WEARING IT WHEN HE WAS CAPTURED BY BISTECO!
DADDY!
MY SON!!
DADDY! I NEVER KNEW WHO MY FATHER WAS! THE APACHES WHO RAISED ME NEVER TOLD ME WHERE I WAS FROM! SO, I'M NOT APACHE?
NO, MY BOY. DO YOU REMEMBER THE SONGS YOUR MOTHER USED TO SING TO YOU?...
THIS LULLABY: "SLEEP, BABY MINE THE SETTING SUN DOTH SHINE..."
41 A
"...UPON THE GREEN HILLS SMILING DOWN ON LONDONDERRY TOWN..."
LISTEN, HOW ABOUT ASKING THE KID TO PUT OUT THE TORCH? KIDS SHOULDN'T BE ALLOWED TO PLAY WITH FIRE!
THIS DOESN'T CHANGE ANYTHING! MEDICINE MAN ADMITS HE'S A PALEFACE. MEDICINE MAN WILL BURN AT STAKE TOO!
DADDY!
MONSTER! YOU SHALL NOT HARM ONE FEATHER OF MY SON'S HEAD!
PATRONIMO DOES WHAT HE LIKES, SEE?
PATRONIMO FORGETS THAT I'M THE BLOOD BROTHER OF HIS FATHER, BISTECO!
YEAH. YOU WOULDN'T WANT TO DO ANYTHING NASTY TO YOUR BLOOD UNCLE!
I HOPE I'M NOT EENTERRUPTING ANYTHING, AMIGOS?
41 B

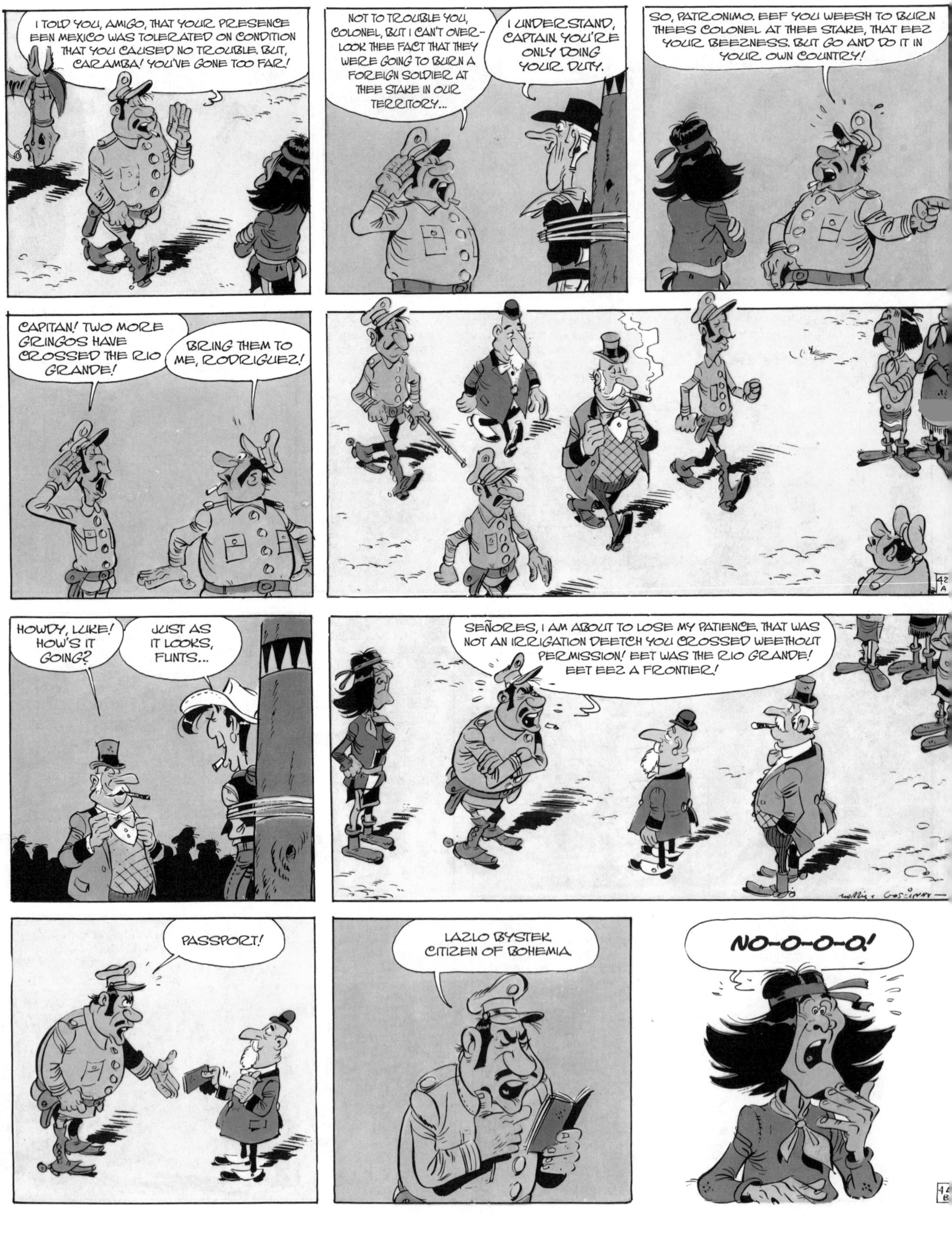
I TOLD YOU, AMIGO, THAT YOUR PRESENCE EEN MEXICO WAS TOLERATED ON CONDITION THAT YOU CAUSED NO TROUBLE. BUT, CARAMBA! YOU'VE GONE TOO FAR!
NOT TO TROUBLE YOU, COLONEL, BUT I CAN'T OVER-LOOK THEE FACT THAT THEY WERE GOING TO BURN A FOREIGN SOLDIER AT THEE STAKE IN OUR TERRITORY...
I UNDERSTAND, CAPTAIN. YOU'RE ONLY DOING YOUR DUTY.
SO, PATRONIMO. EEF YOU WEESH TO BURN THEES COLONEL AT THEE STAKE, THAT EEZ YOUR BEEZNESS. BUT GO AND DO IT IN YOUR OWN COUNTRY!
CAPITAN! TWO MORE GRINGOS HAVE CROSSED THE RIO GRANDE!
BRING THEM TO ME, RODRIGUEZ!
HOWDY, LUKE! HOW'S IT GOING?
JUST AS IT LOOKS, FLINTS...
SEÑORES, I AM ABOUT TO LOSE MY PATIENCE. THAT WAS NOT AN IRRIGATION DEETCH YOU CROSSED WEETHOUT PERMISSION! EET WAS THE RIO GRANDE! EET EEZ A FRONTIER!
PASSPORT!
LAZLO BYSTEK CITIZEN OF BOHEMIA.
NO-O-O-O!

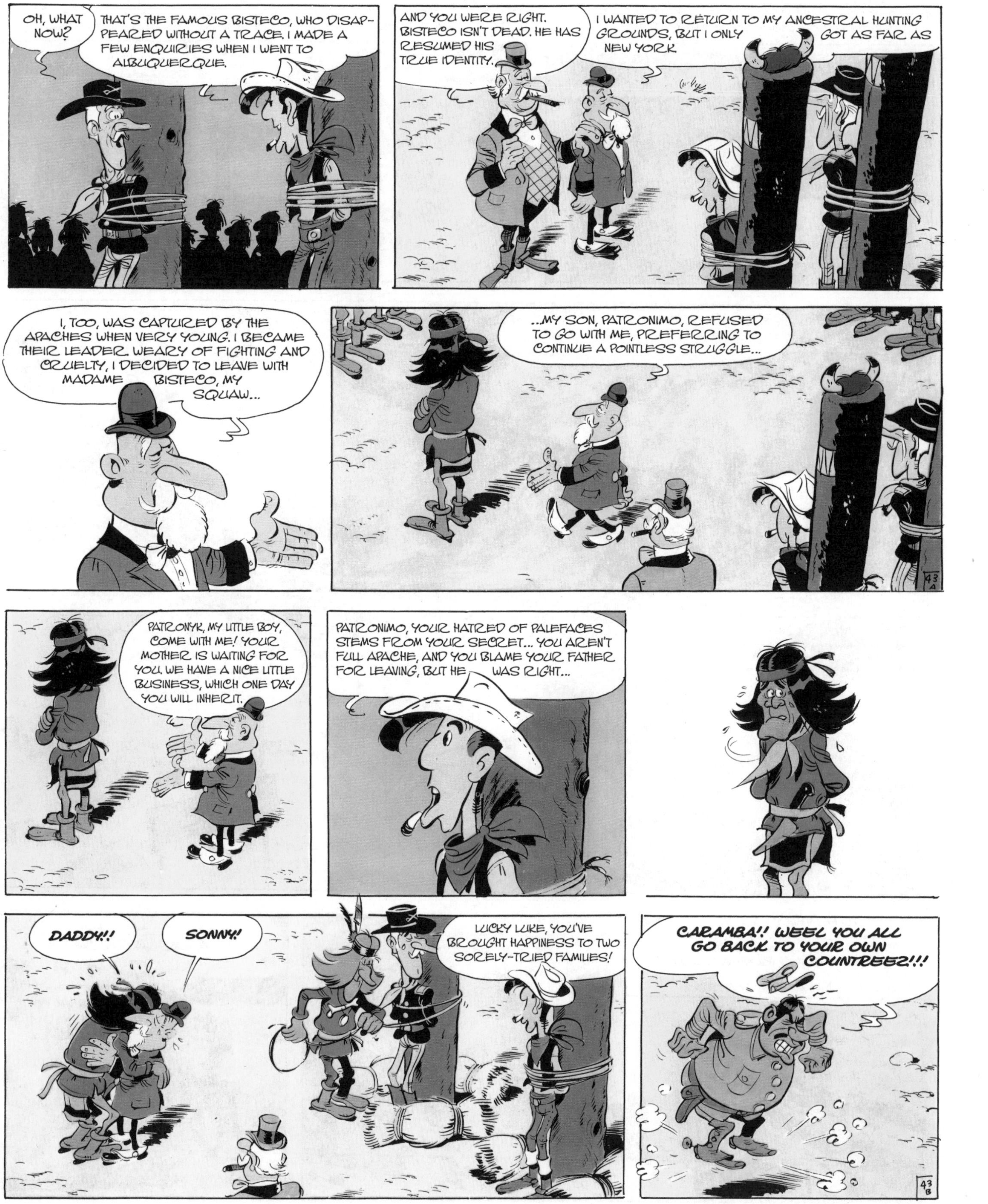
OH, WHAT NOW?
THAT'S THE FAMOUS BISTECO, WHO DISAPPEARED WITHOUT A TRACE. I MADE A FEW ENQUIRIES WHEN I WENT TO ALBUQUERQUE.
AND YOU WERE RIGHT. BISTECO ISN'T DEAD. HE HAS RESUMED HIS TRUE IDENTITY.
I WANTED TO RETURN TO MY ANCESTRAL HUNTING GROUNDS, BUT I ONLY GOT AS FAR AS NEW YORK
I, TOO, WAS CAPTURED BY THE APACHES WHEN VERY YOUNG. I BECAME THEIR LEADER. WEARY OF FIGHTING AND CRUELTY, I DECIDED TO LEAVE WITH MADAME BISTECO, MY SQUAW...
...MY SON, PATRONIMO, REFUSED TO GO WITH ME, PREFERRING TO CONTINUE A POINTLESS STRUGGLE...
PATRONYK, MY LITTLE BOY, COME WITH ME! YOUR MOTHER IS WAITING FOR YOU. WE HAVE A NICE LITTLE BUSINESS, WHICH ONE DAY YOU WILL INHERIT.
PATRONIMO, YOUR HATRED OF PALEFACES STEMS FROM YOUR SECRET... YOU AREN'T FULL APACHE, AND YOU BLAME YOUR FATHER FOR LEAVING, BUT HE WAS RIGHT...
DADDY!!
SONNY!
LUCKY LUKE, YOU'VE BROUGHT HAPPINESS TO TWO SORELY-TRIED FAMILIES!
CARAMBA!! WEEL YOU ALL GO BACK TO YOUR OWN COUNTREEZ!!!

THE WISE ADVICE OF BRAVE CAPTAIN GONZALEZ WAS TAKEN BY EVERY ONE OF THE PROTAGONISTS OF THIS ADVENTURE. PATRONIMO LEFT FOR NEW YORK WITH HIS FATHER.

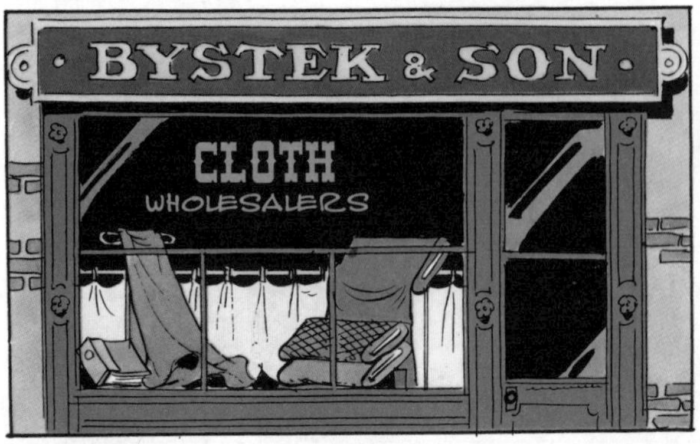
BYSTEK & SON
CLOTH
WHOLESALERS

COLONEL O'NOLLAN RESIGNED FROM THE ARMY AND RETURNED TO IRELAND WITH HIS SON TO REJOIN HIS WIFE. PATRICK O'NOLLAN BECAME A FAMOUS SURGEON, AND ONLY THE KEENEST OBSERVERS COULD DETECT ANY TRACES OF HIS PAST...

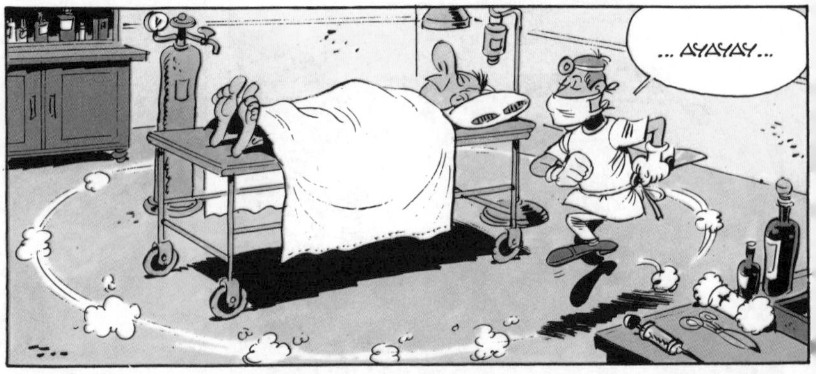
... AYAYAY...

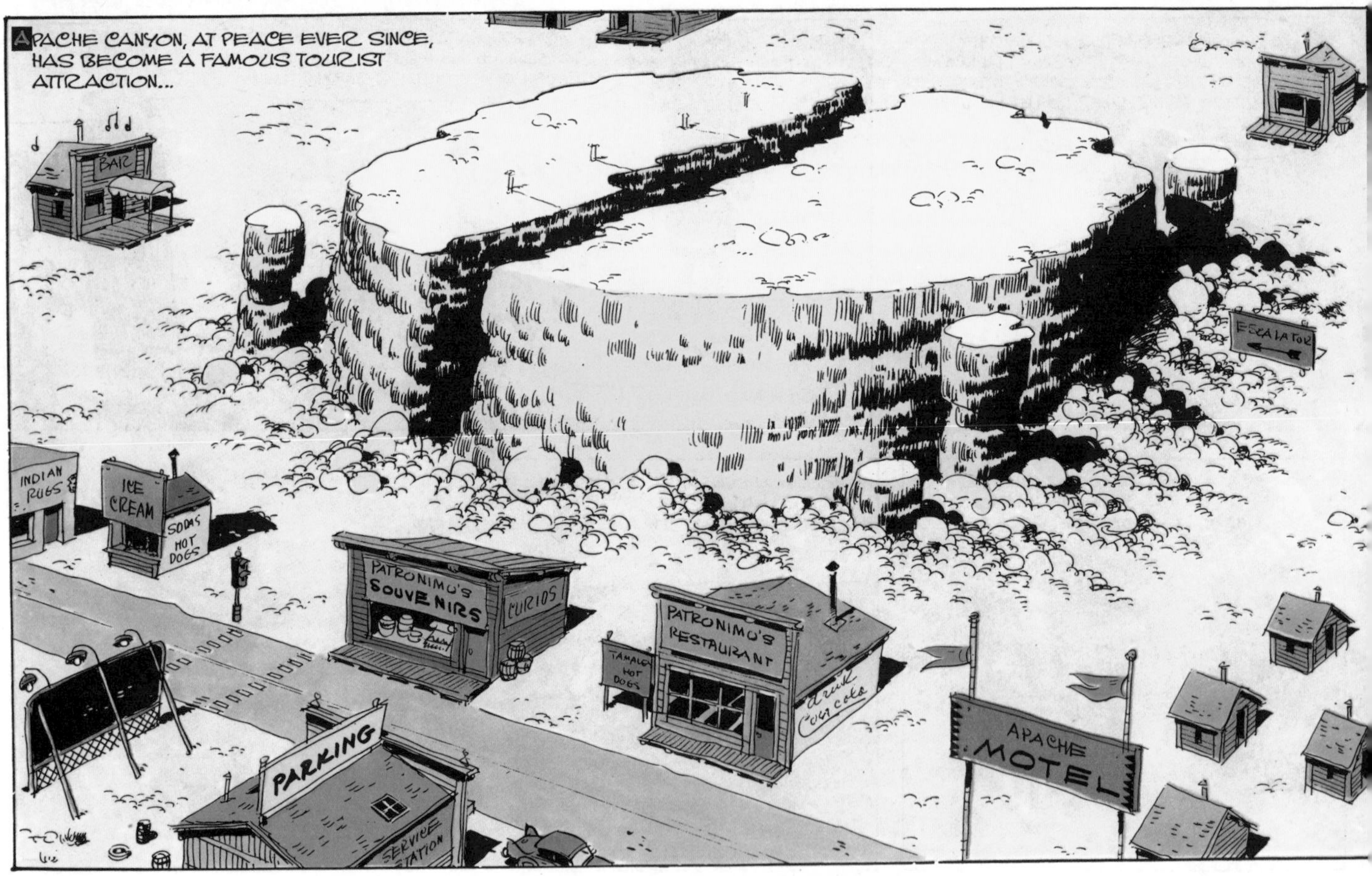
APACHE CANYON, AT PEACE EVER SINCE, HAS BECOME A FAMOUS TOURIST ATTRACTION...
BAR
ESCALATOR
INDIAN RUGS
ICE CREAM
SODAS HOT DOGS
PATRONIMO'S SOUVENIRS
CURIOS
PATRONIMO'S RESTAURANT
TAMALES HOT DOGS
drink Coca cola
APACHE MOTEL
PARKING
SERVICE STATION

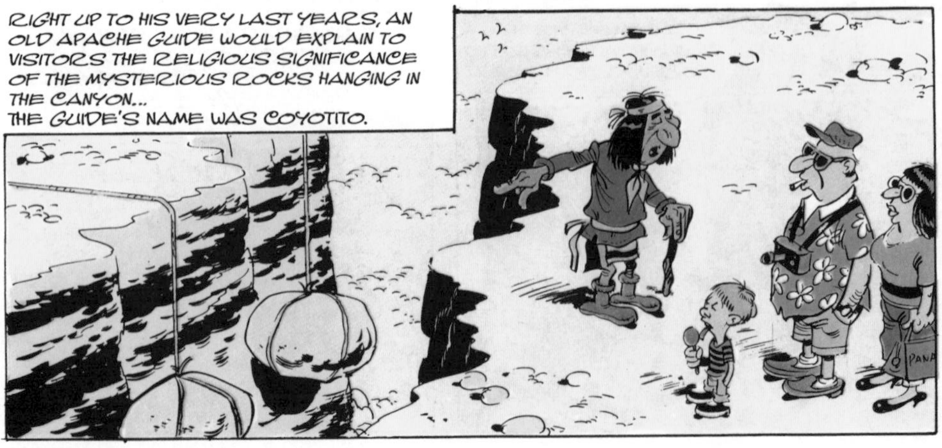
RIGHT UP TO HIS VERY LAST YEARS, AN OLD APACHE GUIDE WOULD EXPLAIN TO VISITORS THE RELIGIOUS SIGNIFICANCE OF THE MYSTERIOUS ROCKS HANGING IN THE CANYON...
THE GUIDE'S NAME WAS COYOTITO.

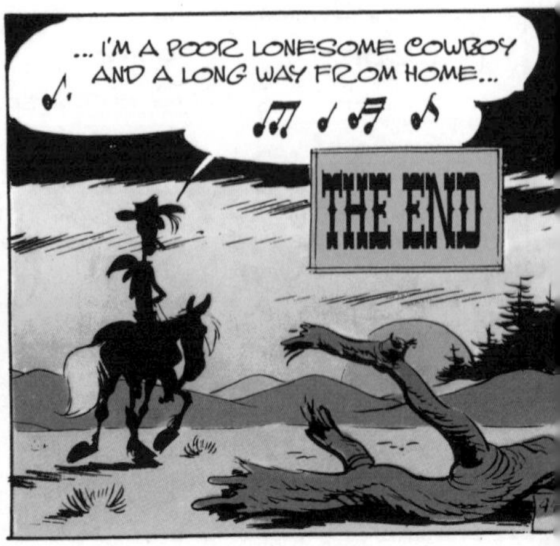
... I'M A POOR LONESOME COWBOY AND A LONG WAY FROM HOME...
THE END

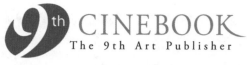

CINEBOOK
The 9th Art Publisher

presents

LUCKY LUKE

The man who shoots faster than his own shadow

A LUCKY LUKE ADVENTURE 1
BILLY the Kid
MORRIS & GOSCINNY
CINEBOOK

A LUCKY LUKE ADVENTURE 2
GHOST TOWN
MORRIS & GOSCINNY
CINEBOOK

A LUCKY LUKE ADVENTURE 3
DALTON CITY
MORRIS & GOSCINNY
CINEBOOK

A LUCKY LUKE ADVENTURE 4
JESSE JAMES
MORRIS & GOSCINNY
CINEBOOK

A LUCKY LUKE ADVENTURE 5
IN THE SHADOW OF THE DERRICKS
E. L. DRAKE OIL CO.
MORRIS & GOSCINNY
CINEBOOK

A LUCKY LUKE ADVENTURE 6
MA DALTON
MORRIS & GOSCINNY
WANTED
DALTON brothers
CINEBOOK

A LUCKY LUKE ADVENTURE 7
BARBED WIRE ON THE PRAIRIE
MORRIS & GOSCINNY
CINEBOOK

A LUCKY LUKE ADVENTURE 8
CALAMITY JANE
MORRIS & GOSCINNY
CINEBOOK

A LUCKY LUKE ADVENTURE 9
THE WAGON TRAIN
MORRIS & GOSCINNY
CINEBOOK

A LUCKY LUKE ADVENTURE 10
TORTILLAS FOR THE DALTONS
MORRIS & GOSCINNY
CINEBOOK

A LUCKY LUKE ADVENTURE 11
WESTERN CIRCUS
MORRIS & GOSCINNY
CINEBOOK

A LUCKY LUKE ADVENTURE 12
THE RIVALS OF PAINFUL GULCH
MORRIS & GOSCINNY
CINEBOOK

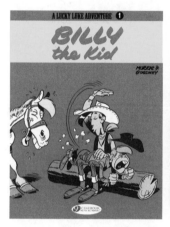

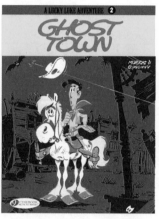

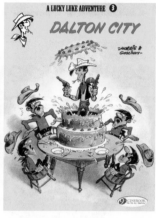

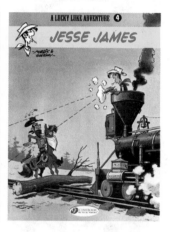

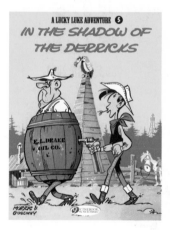

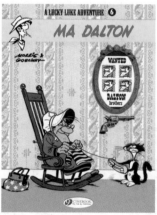

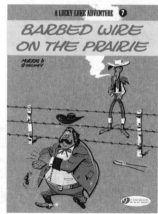

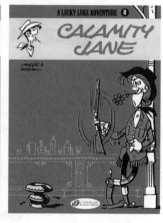

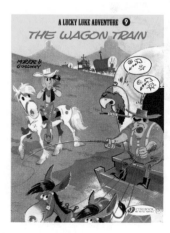

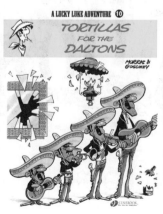

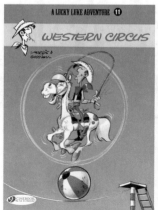

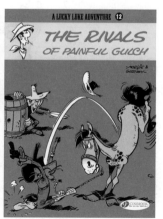

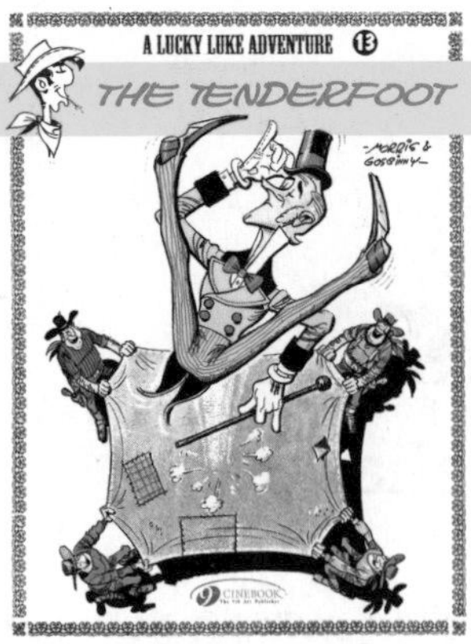
A LUCKY LUKE ADVENTURE 13
THE TENDERFOOT
MORRIS & GOSCINNY
CINEBOOK

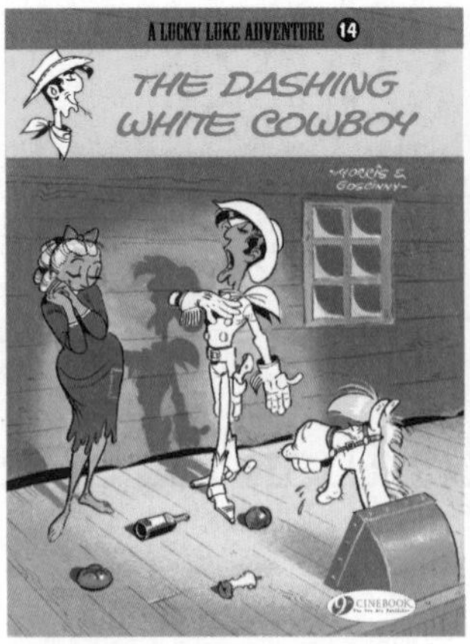
A LUCKY LUKE ADVENTURE 14
THE DASHING WHITE COWBOY
MORRIS & GOSCINNY
CINEBOOK

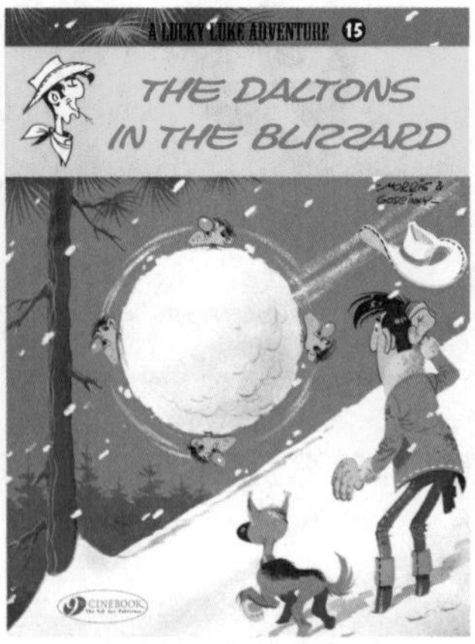
A LUCKY LUKE ADVENTURE 15
THE DALTONS IN THE BLIZZARD
CINEBOOK

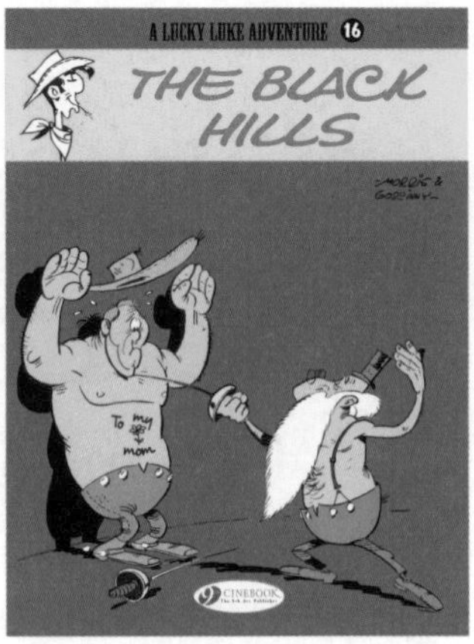
A LUCKY LUKE ADVENTURE 16
THE BLACK HILLS
MORRIS & GOSCINNY
CINEBOOK

COMING SOON

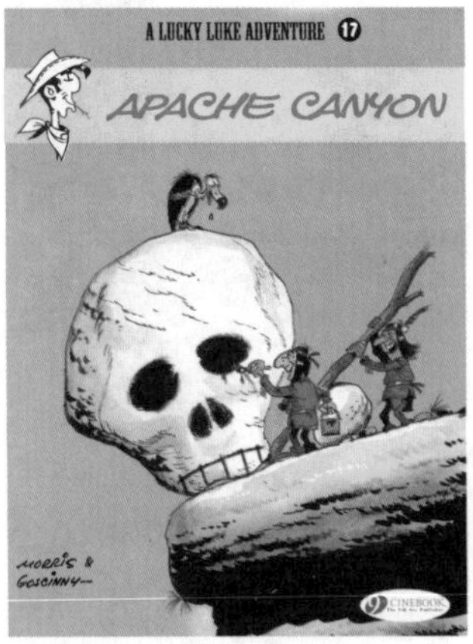
A LUCKY LUKE ADVENTURE 17
APACHE CANYON
MORRIS & GOSCINNY
CINEBOOK

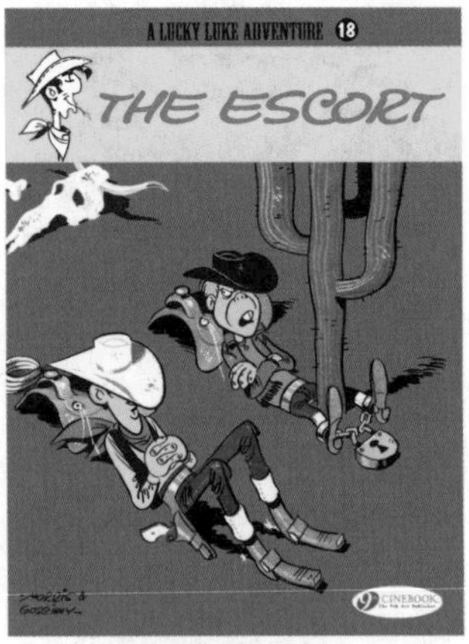
A LUCKY LUKE ADVENTURE 18
THE ESCORT
MORRIS & GOSCINNY
CINEBOOK

AUGUST 2009

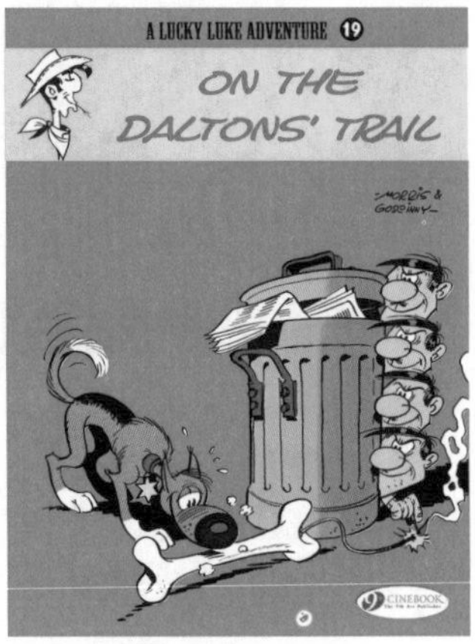
A LUCKY LUKE ADVENTURE 19
ON THE DALTONS' TRAIL
MORRIS & GOSCINNY
CINEBOOK

OCTOBER 2009

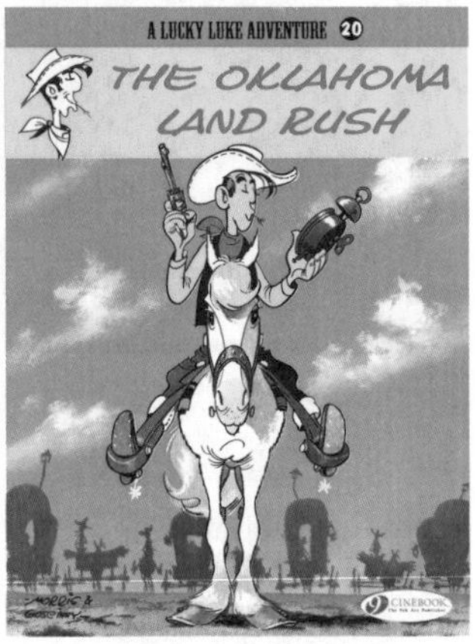
A LUCKY LUKE ADVENTURE 20
THE OKLAHOMA LAND RUSH
MORRIS & GOSCINNY
CINEBOOK

DECEMBER 2009

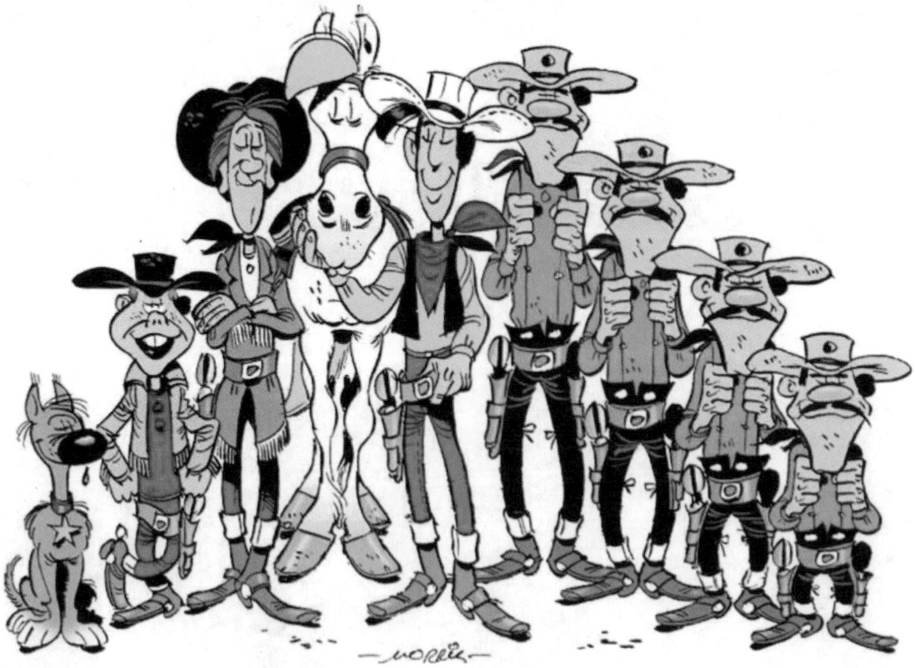
MORRIS

GREYSCALE

BIN TRAVELER FORM

Cut By _Brigum_   Qty _35_   Date _11-04-24_

Scanned By _____ Qty _____ Date _____

Scanned Batch IDs

_____ _____ _____

Notes / Exception

_____

_____

_____

_____

_____